HERE·BE·MONSTERS!

BOOK

CHEESE GALORE!

OXFORD

To Edward, and with enormous thanks
to everyone who has helped along the way

OXFORD
UNIVERSITY PRESS

Great Clarendon Street, Oxford OX2 6DP

Oxford University Press is a department of the University of Oxford.
It furthers the University's objective of excellence in research, scholarship,
and education by publishing worldwide in

Oxford   New York

Auckland   Cape Town   Dar es Salaam   Hong Kong   Karachi
Kuala Lumpur   Madrid   Melbourne   Mexico City   Nairobi
New Delhi   Shanghai   Taipei   Toronto

With offices in

Argentina   Austria   Brazil   Chile   Czech Republic   France   Greece
Guatemala   Hungary   Italy   Japan   Poland   Portugal   Singapore
South Korea   Switzerland   Thailand   Turkey   Ukraine   Vietnam

Oxford is a registered trade mark of Oxford University Press
in the UK and in certain other countries

Text and illustrations © Alan Snow 2005

The moral rights of the author have been asserted

Database right Oxford University Press (maker)

First published 2005 as part of *Here Be Monsters!*
First published in this paperback edition 2008

British Library Cataloguing in Publication Data

Data available

ISBN: 978-0-19-275542-1

1 3 5 7 9 10 8 6 4 2

Printed in Great Britain by Cox & Wyman Ltd, Reading, Berkshire.

CONTENTS

Johnson's Taxonomy
of Trolls and Creatures

Aardvark
Aardvarks are invariably the first animals listed in any alphabetical listing of creatures. Beyond this they have few attributes relevant here.

Boxtrolls
A sub-species of the common troll, they are very shy, so live inside a box. These they gather from the backs of large shops. They are somewhat troublesome creatures–as they have a passion for everything mechanical and no understanding of the concept of ownership (they steal anything which is not bolted down, and more often than not, anything which is). It is very dangerous to leave tools lying about where they might find them.

Cabbageheads
Belief has it that cabbageheads live deep underground and are the bees of the underworld. Little else is known at this time, apart from a fondness for brassicas.

Cheese
Wild English Cheeses live in bogs. This is unlike their French cousins who live in caves. They are nervous beasties, that eat grass by night, in the meadows and woodlands. They are also of very low intelligence, and are panicked by almost anything that catches them unawares. Cheeses make easy quarry for hunters, being rather easier to catch than a dead sheep.

Crow
The crow is a very intelligent bird, capable of living in many environments. Crows are known to be considerably more honest than their cousins, magpies, and enjoy a varied diet, and good company. Usually they are charming company, but should be kept from providing the entertainment. Failure to do so may result in tedium, for while intelligent, crows seem to lack taste in the choice of music, and conversational topics.

Fresh-water Sea-cow
Distant relative of the manitou. This creature inhabits the canals, and drains of certain West Country towns. A passive creature of large size, and vegetarian habits. They are very kind to their young, and make good mothers.

Grandfather (William)

Arthur's guardian and carer. Grandfather has lived underground for many years in a cave home where he pursues his interests in engineering. All the years in a damp cave have taken their toll, and he now suffers from very bad rheumatism, and a somewhat short temper.

The Man in the Iron Socks

A mysterious shadowy figure said to be much feared by the members of the now defunct Cheese Guild. He is thought to hold a dark secret as well as a large 'Walloper'. His Walloper is the major cause of fear, but he also has a sharp tongue, and a caustic line in wit. History does not relate the reasoning behind his wearing of iron socks.

The Members

Members of the secretive Ratbridge Cheese Guild, that was thought to have died out after the 'Great Cheese Crash'. It was an evil organization that rigged the cheese market, and doctored and adulterated lactose-based food stuffs.

Rabbits

Furry, jumping mammals, with a passion for tender vegetables and raising the young. Good parents, but not very bright.

Rabbit Women

Very little is known about these mythical creatures, except that they are supposed to live with rabbits, and wear clothes spun from rabbit wool.

Rats

Rats are known to be some of the most intelligent of all rodents, and to be considerably more intelligent than many humans. They are known to have a passion for travel, and be extremely adaptable. They often live in a symbiotic relationship with humans.

Trotting Badgers

Trotting badgers are some of the nastiest creatures to be found anywhere. With their foul temper, rapid speed, and razor-sharp teeth, it cannot be stressed just how unpleasant and dangerous these creatures are. It is only their disgusting stench that gives warning of their proximity, and when smelt it is often too late.

The Story So Far . . .

TRAPPED!

ARTHUR has lived all his life in the Underworld, deep below the streets of Ratbridge, with his grandfather, and only comes above ground occasionally. But now Arthur is trapped above ground, thanks to the dastardly Archibald Snatcher and his men, who have stolen his mechanical wings and sealed all the entrances into the Underworld.

Snatcher, surrounded by hounds, stood by the drain cover

Arthur joined Willbury and the group of creatures

HERE BE MONSTERS!

ARTHUR takes refuge with Willbury Nibble in his disued pet shop. There he meets boxtrolls and a cabbagehead, who quickly become his firm friends.

SOME RATHER SMALL CREATURES

A sinister visitor, Mr Gristle, comes to the pet shop and sells Willbury a miniature boxtroll, cabbagehead, and sea-cow. Later, in the market, Arthur and Willbury see more mysterious tiny creatures, sold by the bizarre Madame Froufrou.

Madame Froufrou passed the tiny boxtroll down to the lady

MARJORIE

HOPING that Willbury's friend Marjorie can help them find Arthur's wings, Arthur and Willbury go to find her at the patent hall. She is extremely upset as she has invented something wonderful—too secret to tell them about—and her invention has been stolen by an unscrupulous father and son, Louis and Edward Trout.

A very upset Marjorie

GONE!

TOGETHER the friends return home, but find that a disaster awaits them. While they were out, the pet shop has been ransacked—and all the big creatures have been stolen! As they stand wondering what to do, a sailor called Kipper and a rat called Tom arrive, from the Ratbridge Nautical Laundry.

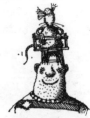

'Good morning! Need any washing done?'

SKULDUGGERY!

'Something has got to be done!'

TOM and Kipper tell them that some rats have gone missing from the Laundry, too—and they suspect that some shady characters from the Cheese Hall are responsible—including Snatcher and Gristle! Everyone decides they must work together to find out what is going on, and to get their friends back, and so they set off for the Nautical Laundry to make a plan . . .

CABBAGEHEADS

MEANWHILE, we discover that the Underworld has started to flood. A colony of cabbageheads is forced to move to look for drier ground. But they stumble into a terrible trap . . .

Caught in a net and collected by a group of men wearing tall hats

INTO THE CHEESE HALL

'Back to the laundry! Follow us!'

ARTHUR, Willbury, Marjorie and the sailors and rats go to stake out the Cheese Hall. Arthur, defying Willbury's instructions, manages to sneak inside. There, in a deep dungeon, he finds the creatures imprisoned. After much danger, Arthur finds his wings, and manages to escape with the creatures.

THE DASTARDLY PLAN

BACK at the laundry, some policemen arrive. Clearly in the thrall of Snatcher, they arrest Arthur and send him back to the Cheese Hall. There, Snatcher reveals to Arthur that he and his men are using Marjorie's invention—a shrinking machine!—to steal the size from big creatures and turn them into miniature ones. What the reason is he will not say . . .

Arthur alone in the dungeon

THE MAN IN THE IRON SOCKS

IN the dungeon, Arthur makes the acquaintance of the man in the next cell. His name is Herbert and he has been there for many years. He has been given iron socks so that Snatcher's men can control him by turning on a powerful magnet in the roof of his cell.

'So if I cause any trouble . . . they just turn the magnet on . . . boink!'

'They won't bother us if we're dressed as boxtrolls'

THE RESCUE PARTY

MEANWHILE, Willbury and co. finally find a way into the Underworld, by dressing up as boxtrolls to outwit Snatcher's men, and set out to try to rescue Arthur by tunnelling up from below the Cheese Hall. The Underworld is flooding fast and all the underlings—and Grandfather—are in grave danger.

THE TRUTH AT LAST

BACK in the dungeon, Arthur manages to use his special doll to communicate with Grandfather—and discovers that Grandfather and Herbert are very old friends, and that Herbert has something to do with the reason that Arthur and Grandfather live underground. At last Grandfather is ready to tell Arthur the truth . . .

'It's time you heard the truth about why we live underground'

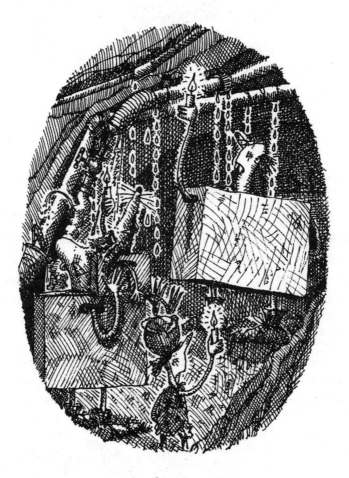

Something was wrong

Fish and the other real boxtrolls had a way of walking
with their feet a few inches up either wall to avoid the water

Chapter 1

WET!

Several inches of water ran down the tunnels as the procession made its way under the town. Fish and the other real boxtrolls had a way of walking with their feet a few inches up either wall to avoid the water, but even so it dripped down from the ceiling onto their boxes. Willbury and the others were getting very, very wet, and the rats were complaining as the water came up well over the bottom of their boxes.

Tom came to a stop and took out his teeth. 'It's not the water that I hate,' said Tom. 'It's the feeling of the soggy cardboard rubbing on my legs. It feels really horrid, like old wellies.'

'It's the feeling of the soggy cardboard rubbing on my legs'

Rats with dripping boxes were lifted, and carried aloft

'We can do something about that,' said Willbury, taking out his teeth. Then he shouted the order: 'Large boxtrolls please pick up small boxtrolls and carry them till it gets drier. And you can remove your teeth till further notice.'

All down the line teeth were removed and rats with dripping boxes were lifted and carried aloft.

'Thanks!' said Tom to Willbury.

The tunnels slowly rose up towards the town, but remained very wet. The real boxtrolls were now in familiar territory, and they didn't need their candles. Fish kept rushing ahead into the darkness and returning excitedly. After a few of these forays he seemed to grow pensive.

'Have you noticed pipes up on the roof?' asked Tom.

Willbury held up his candle to look. There were pipes . . . and most of them were leaking. Something was wrong.

The tunnel levelled out, and Fish led them to an area of what looked like very old cellars. They went in and turned a corner to see an iron ladder fixed to a wall in front of them. The ladder disappeared up into darkness. Fish signalled to them to stop, then went up the ladder followed by the other real boxtrolls. After a few minutes a distressed-looking Fish returned alone.

Willbury spoke. 'What is it, Fish?'

Fish signalled to them to follow him up the ladder.

The group silently followed Fish and after a short climb they came up through a hole on to a dry floor. Wherever they were it was big, as the light from their candles faded into darkness around them. There was a loud click, and above them a light came on. Shoe was standing on top of a huge pile of nuts and bolts, and holding a chain fixed to some kind of glass ball. The light from the ball flooded the cavern. Everywhere there were machine tools, half built pumps, broken bicycles, bits of wire, tools, and pieces of metal of every shape, colour, and description. The place was an Aladdin's cave of engineering scrap.

Shoe was standing on top of a huge pile of nuts and bolts,
and holding a chain fixed to some kind of glass ball

'This is the boxtrolls' nest!' exclaimed Willbury.

The boxtrolls nodded.

Marjorie was staring up at the glowing glass ball. 'They've got electric light! Fancy that. I thought it might be possible one day.'

Willbury looked about. 'Where are the other boxtrolls?'

The real boxtrolls looked very sad and unhappy.

The place was an Aladdin's cave of engineering scrap.

Kipper looked at them and whispered, ' . . . I think Snatcher has taken them . . . '

Willbury took this in, then replied. 'That may be it. But it would mean that he must have been capturing them somehow . . . and down here!'

Fish turned to the boxtrolls that Arthur had freed. They just nodded.

Willbury spoke to them very gently. 'You were captured down here?'

The boxtrolls nodded again, pointed back down the hole, and started burbling.

'Could you show us the way up to the Cheese Hall?'

They shook their heads and mumbled.

Titus whispered to Willbury, then Willbury turned to the others. 'Snatcher and his mob put them in sacks after they were captured. But they think he has some sort of mechanical elevator, with an entrance down here somewhere. They say it shot them up to the Cheese Hall as fast as a rocket.'

'They say it shot them up to the Cheese Hall as fast as a rocket'

'Do you think we could find it?' asked Tom.

The boxtrolls looked unsure, and Titus whispered again to Willbury.

'Titus says that this place is such a warren that the elevator could be hidden anywhere.'

Everybody looked very glum.

Then Willbury spoke again. 'I think we should split up and search for the elevator. It shouldn't take long with so many of us. We'll meet up here in an hour?'

It was agreed, and they split up into small groups and set off. Willbury stayed with Fish, Titus, Tom, and Kipper, while Marjorie teamed up with Shoe, Egg, and some other boxtrolls. As they waited for their turn to descend the ladder, Willbury spoke to his group.

'There is something else I want to do before we start looking for the elevator. I've got to find Arthur's grandfather. I am very concerned, as he must be running out of food.'

Fish perked up and raised a hand.

'Do you know where he lives?' asked Willbury. Fish burbled something and Titus whispered something to Willbury.

'You say you have heard that there are some humans living in a cave off one of the large caverns?'

Fish nodded.

'Do you think you can lead us there?' Fish looked a little unsure, then nodded again.

'Well, let's try that!' said Willbury. And off they set back down the ladder.

And off they set back down the ladder

The Evil Crime

'Don't you remember burning a hole in my mum's carpet with the toy steam engine we tried to build?'

Chapter 2

THE TELLING

In the cell in the dungeon Arthur listened as Grandfather started to talk. 'Herbert. Do you remember growing up?'

'No.' Herbert sounded very sad.

'What? You don't remember anything? Don't you remember the Glue Lane Technical School for the Poor?'

'Not really . . . I do remember the name . . . You're going to have to remind me.'

'Herbert, we grew up in the same street! We played together, got measles together, got in trouble together . . . and got our ears clipped together. Don't you remember burning a hole in my mum's carpet with the toy steam engine we tried to build?'

There was a pause. 'Was the carpet a rather odd green colour?'

'Yes! Yes it was!'

'I do remember something . . .'

*'Do you remember us sinking in the canal up to our
waists when we tried to cross it when it was frozen?'*

'Do you remember us sinking in the canal up to our
waists when we tried to cross it when it was frozen?'

'And the ice was so thin in the middle that it cracked and
your dad had to pull us out?'

'Yes!'

' . . . It is coming back to me . . . remind me more,'
Herbert said.

'Do you remember Tuesday mornings with the smell of
the brewery? And cold nights in winter when the smell of
the tannery filled the streets?'

'I loved the smell of the brewery, but the tannery smelt
awful!'

'You are not wrong there!'

At first Arthur somehow felt that it was not his place to
be involved in the conversation, but now he asked a
question.

'I know there is a tannery, but a brewery?'

'Not any more. It went the same time as the Cheese
Industry . . . with the pollution.'

'What happened?'

'Ratbridge was founded on the cheese, but when new industries came to the town, the smoke and waste they produced poisoned the water supply and a lot of countryside around here. It got so bad that the local cheeses were decreed unfit to eat, and the cheese industry collapsed. The Cheese Barons went bankrupt overnight.'

'The Cheese Barons went bankrupt overnight'

'I think I remember that . . . ' Herbert said. 'Ain't that the reason that Archibald Snatcher turned up at the Poor School?'

'Yes,' replied Grandfather. 'His father was partly responsible for the ban.'

'Why?' asked Arthur.

'He ran a mill that had always produced really dodgy cheese. They used all kinds of evil processes. One of their tricks was to boil down cheese rinds, extract the oil, and then inject it into immature cheeses. It was illegal . . . and cruel, but they had got away with it. What they didn't realize was that as the pollution got worse, making cheese oil was concentrating the poisons. Finally they got sued when they produced the cheese that poisoned the Duchess of

Snookworth . . . and it was her husband who got the ban brought in. Archibald's dad lost his fortune and couldn't afford to have dear Archibald privately tutored any more.'

'Oh, I remember Snatcher turning up at school now!' Herbert's memory was coming back. 'He didn't take his fall from Ratbridge society well. Hateful little snob!'

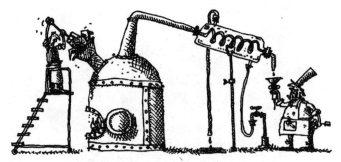

'One of their tricks was to boil down cheese rinds, extract the oil, and then inject it into immature cheeses'

Grandfather continued. 'Herbert and I were in our third year at school when Archibald turned up. He had spent his whole life being waited on hand and foot, so poverty came as a bit of a shock to him. He hated the school, and everybody in it . . . including us!'

'Why?' asked Arthur.

'He thought it was his rightful place to do what he wanted, and never lift a finger . . . but we didn't play that game,' said Herbert. 'He loathed us and everybody else. He seemed to think that Ratbridge had done him out of his rightful fortune, and his resentment turned to cheating and stealing.'

Grandfather went on, 'But, oh, he was cunning! Over the next few years Archibald took every opportunity that came his way to advance himself back towards his "rightful place". Smarming up to the teachers, borrowing work, a little blackmail, some bullying, and extortion. When it came to the final exam results it was no surprise that he got the highest results . . . '

'When it came to the final exam results it was no surprise that he got the highest results . . . '

'Because he stole them!' interjected Herbert.

'On the strength of a bit of blackmail, and his stolen results, he got a scholarship to Oxford. And that was the last we heard of him for a few years, till . . . ' Grandfather's voice sounded bitter. 'Do you remember now, Herbert, what happened?'

'At the inn?' Herbert replied, slowly.

'Yes, at the inn.'

'Yes . . . some of it is coming back.'

'What did happen?' asked Arthur.

'Herbert and I had just set up as freelance inventors and engineers. We worked in the factories for years, but we had managed to save up enough to start a small workshop, and the work was coming in . . . Then one lunchtime we went to the Nag's Head. We were just setting about a couple of large pasties when we heard a raised voice at the next table. I looked over, and there sat Mr Archibald Snatcher flanked by a couple of heavies.

' "Are you calling me a cheat, sir?" he said to a red-faced man across the table from him.

' "Yes, sir, I am," said the red-faced man. "It is not possible to have a hand of cards containing seven aces!"

' "It is, sir, for I am very lucky!" Archibald said.

' "Well, today, sir, your luck has run out!" And the man at the other end of the table reached inside his pocket. Thinking he was going for a gun, one of the heavies also reached for his pocket, and in an instant the bar cleared, leaving just Herbert and me watching the altercation.'

'It is not possible to have a hand of cards containing seven aces!'

'Oh, yes!' broke in Herbert. 'The man took out a note-pad and asked for Snatcher's name and address. He wanted to report him to the police . . . But he didn't notice that one of Snatcher's men had taken out a catapult . . . '

Herbert fell silent again, and Grandfather continued.

'That's right,' he said. 'And that's when Snatcher gave the order to the heavy with the catapult . . .

'And that's when Snatcher gave the order to the heavy with the catapult . . . '

' "Administer the treatment!" he said. There was a blur and something green whizzed across the table and struck the red-faced man in the mouth. The man went pale and slumped to the floor. Then we caught the smell. Oil of Brussels!'

'What's Oil of Brussels?' asked Arthur.

'It is poison distilled from sprouts. It is very fast acting, and often lethal. Later I found out they had shot a small wad of cotton soaked in it down the man's throat,' replied Grandfather.

'It is poison distilled from sprouts. It is very fast acting, and often lethal.'

'Awful!' added Herbert.

Grandfather went on, 'Then there was the sound of police whistles outside, and Snatcher saw us.'

' "Oh, look! A couple of old school friends," he said. Then he reached inside a pocket and threw something to me. The very moment I caught it, the bar door swung open, and a group of Squeakers ran in and saw the man slumped on the floor. Then Snatcher stood up, and pointed at me.

'Then he reached inside a pocket and threw something to me'

' "It was him, officer! He has just poisoned that man. Look! He is still holding the evidence." I looked down . . . and in my hand was a bottle of Oil of Brussels.

' "Arrest that man!" shouted one of the Squeakers, and they rushed to get me. So I panicked and made a run for it straight through the back door to the street. The Squeakers followed me, but I was quite fit in those days and I managed to shake them off and climbed down a drain . . . '

'I managed to shake them off and climbed down a drain . . . '

'I remember!' cried Herbert. 'You ran out of the door with the Squeakers after you, then . . . ' He paused for a long time, and then whispered, ' . . . everything went green . . . and I woke up here.'

'Everything went green . . . '

'How do you think you got here?' Arthur asked him.

'They must have knocked me out or something, then kidnapped me . . . ' muttered Herbert.

'I knew you had disappeared, because that night I came up out of the drain and found posters up for our arrest for attempted murder. I just didn't know where you had gone. I grabbed some food from a garden, then went back underground to avoid being caught. I knew I would never be safe above ground again unless I could find you as a witness to the truth.'

'Attempted murder? So the man wasn't dead?' asked Arthur.

'No, he survived, but he suffered from permanent memory loss of the event, due to the poison and trauma.'

'That's why everything went green. They must have had some more Oil of Brussels and smothered me with it. That's why me memory is so bad!' said Herbert sounding furious. 'And I guess we've both been prisoners of sorts ever since . . . '

'Yes . . . Yes . . . it is true,' replied Grandfather. 'Mr Archibald Snatcher has a lot to answer for.'

'So can you help us, William?' Herbert started to ask. But before Grandfather could reply, Arthur heard footsteps coming down the steps to the dungeon.

'Quick! Someone is coming. I'll speak to you later, Grandfather.' He tucked the doll inside his suit, pushed the stone back in its hole and pushed the bed against the wall. The footsteps approached, and a Member appeared carrying a bowl in one hand and a cudgel in the other.

'The guv sent me down 'ere with some nosh for you.' He put the plate down, took a key from his pocket, and unlocked the door to Arthur's cell. Then he slid the plate into the cell with his foot and closed and locked the door.

'Take your time, boy! I got to wait for the plate, but I'm in no hurry. They ain't going to be back from the traps for ages.' He sat down, leant against the bars of the cell opposite, and started to watch Arthur eat.

*The footsteps approached, and a Member appeared carrying
a bowl in one hand and a cudgel in the other*

They saw a small window in a wall of rock ahead

'It's rhubarb! We must be getting close!'

Chapter 3

A Glimmer at the End of the Tunnel

Fish led the way, and as they walked water washed around their feet. The water level seemed to be rising all the time. Then a smell gently wafted into their noses. It was sweet and vaguely familiar. Something about it reminded Willbury of jam. They'd not eaten for a long time and the smell was almost too much to bear.

Willbury stopped. 'That's it! It's rhubarb! We must be getting close!'

After a few bends in the pathway, a light became visible. Over the rush of water they could just hear music. Then they saw a small window in a wall of rock ahead. As they got closer, the music grew louder, and next to the window a door became visible. They reached the door and Willbury knocked.

The music stopped, there was some muttering, and the door swung open to reveal a short stocky old man with a huge beard and glasses. He looked very damp.

'My word! You're big for a boxtroll!' Grandfather said.

Willbury had completely forgotten he was in disguise and was rather suprised.

'My word! You're big for a boxtroll!'

'I am not a boxtroll!'

'Well, you will do until a boxtroll comes along. I have something I need you to help me with—urgently!'

'Of course, we will do anything we can to help. I have spoken to you before, sir. I am Willbury Nibble.'

'Oh! I thought you were a lawyer, not a boxtroll! It just shows that you shouldn't jump to conclusions. But I am pleased to meet you anyway,' said Grandfather, looking surprised.

'It's a disguise,' said Willbury. 'I *am* a lawyer. And I'm afraid I have some rather bad news for you about Arthur.'

'I spoke to him just a little while ago,' said Grandfather. 'He managed to call me from the dungeon at the Cheese Hall. We have to do something to help him before it's too late.'

'That is why we are here,' said Willbury. 'We believe there is a way up into the Cheese Hall from the Underworld. If only we can find it, we can make our way up into the Hall and help Arthur escape.'

'I see,' said Grandfather thoughtfully. 'I don't know of any such way—but there may be one . . . I also have an idea of how to help Arthur—but I can't do it on my own. I've been hoping for some underlings to come along and help me, but they seem few and far between these days. But perhaps you and your friends can make it work.'

'Of course we will do anything we can. Arthur is our friend and we all want to get him back as soon as we can.'

'Well, do come in,' Grandfather said, taking a step back and gesturing Willbury into his home. 'And bring your friends.'

'Thank you!' said Willbury, and they followed Grandfather in.

'The more the merrier!' said Grandfather. 'If you all like stewed rhubarb I think I might have just enough to go round. Please help yourselves,' he said, pointing to a saucepan on an old range. 'Then I would appreciate it if you would come through to the back room. I need some help.'

There was a cheer and they set about serving up the rhubarb. Very soon it was all gone and they followed

Grandfather into the back room of the cave. There were puddles on the floor and water was dripping from the ceiling.

'If you all like stewed rhubarb I think I might have just enough to go round.'

The small room was about the most crowded Willbury had ever seen. At its centre was a brass bedstead. This was covered in a beautiful patchwork quilt. Surrounding the bed was a huge hotch-potch of wires, rods, cogs, pulleys, and other things that Willbury couldn't identify.

'Er . . . What is it?' he asked.

'It's something I have been working on for years. It's finished, but I am too frail to operate it. I just spoke to Arthur and he desperately needs help. I think this is the only way we may be able to get him out of his situation.'

Grandfather explained his machine.

'It sounds amazing!' declared Willbury. 'I only wish Marjorie was here to see it . . . But I certainly think we can help—obviously we need real muscle and some brains here,' he continued, smiling at Kipper and Tom. 'And I know just the pirate and rat for the job!'

Grandfather followed Willbury's gaze. 'Are you sure, Mr Nibble?'

Surrounding the bed was a huge hotch-potch of wires, rods, cogs, pulleys, and other things

Arthur in the dungeon

He used his fingers to scrape it off the surface of the bowl

Chapter 4

THE KEYS

Arthur was very hungry and even though the cold porridge in his bowl was almost solid, he tried to eat it. He'd not been given a spoon so he used his fingers to scrape it off the surface of the bowl. It was a very slow process. As he ate his gaoler slowly drifted off to sleep.

'I give up!' Arthur muttered eventually. 'I think I'd rather starve.'

He looked over at the gaoler, who was now fast asleep and starting to snore. Arthur coughed loudly, but the gaoler didn't stir. Encouraged by this, he put the plate down slowly on the floor, reached under his suit, and retrieved his doll. Glancing nervously at the sleeping gaoler, he quietly wound the handle, and whispered into the doll.

'Grandfather! Keep your voice down! There's one of Snatcher's mob just outside the cell . . . asleep.'

'What's he doing there?' came a quiet voice from the doll.

The gaoler didn't stir

'He just brought me some food.'

'Did he have to unlock your cell?'

'Yes . . . Why?'

'So he's got a key?

'Yes.'

'Well, this might just be our lucky day. Where's the key?'

'It's in his right-hand coat pocket,' Arthur whispered. 'But how are we going to get it off him? He's right across the corridor, and there is no way I can reach him.'

'Listen, Arthur. I have a plan, but you need to do exactly as I say. I want you to wind up the doll till you hear it ping . . . then give the handle a few more turns until you feel the clockwork can't take any more. But be very careful and don't break the spring!'

Arthur carefully did what he was told, and wound it very gently till there was a ping. The noise made him jump, and he turned to check it hadn't disturbed the sleeping gaoler.

Then he carefully wound the handle a few more times until he felt it couldn't go any further.

Arthur wound it very gently till there was a ping

'OK, I've wound it up.'

'Right,' said Grandfather. 'Reach out of your cell as far as you can, and stand the doll up, facing towards the pocket with the keys in.'

Arthur was puzzled, but did what he was told.

In Grandfather's bedroom underground, Kipper and Tom were ready. Kipper sat on a bicycle that had had its back wheel removed and replaced with some kind of complicated pump. But Tom was involved in something far more complicated. He was at the centre of a web of levers and wires that stretched out from all over the room. And on his head were a pair of goggles far too large for him. Fixed over the lens of the goggles was a box with wires sprouting from it.

Grandfather turned away from the strange trumpet mouth he had been speaking into, and spoke directly to Tom and Kipper. 'I am really not sure if this is going to work. Can

*Kipper sat on a bicycle that had had its back wheel removed
and replaced with some kind of complicated pump*

you please get ready . . . and remember what I said to you.
You have to work together!'

'Working together is what we do best,' replied Tom from
behind the goggles.

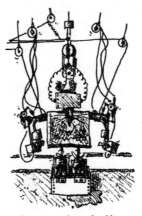

Tom was at the centre of a web of levers and wires

Kipper began to pedal and soon a humming started to
come from the pump, and the levers and wires attached to
Tom went taut.

High above in the dungeon, Arthur stood by the bars and stared down at the doll . . . Something was happening! Arthur heard the ping, and then a slow ticking. The doll's eyes lit up, and cast two small pools of light towards the coat pocket. Then the doll started shaking and fell over.

The doll started shaking and fell over

In Grandfather's bedroom Kipper was working the pedals as hard as he could, and Tom was cursing.

'What's the matter?' asked Grandfather.

'It's fallen over,' said Tom.

'What can you see through the goggles?' asked Grandfather.

'Just the gaoler's boots, at the moment,' replied Tom.

'Use the levers to move the doll's arms. They should be able to help you get it upright again,' instructed Grandfather.

Tom carefully started to move the levers. After a few moments he spoke.

'The doll must be moving! I can see all of the gaoler now.'

'Try moving your legs. The doll should copy your movements.'

Tom felt the wires pull as he started to bend his legs.

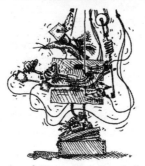

Tom carefully started to move the levers

Arthur watched the doll in amazement as it now started to move its arms. It seemed to be trying to get up on its own!

The doll's legs now moved as well and it managed to stand again. Then its wings unfolded. Suddenly Arthur understood.

'Faster!' Grandfather shouted at Kipper. 'Pedal faster! We need all the power we can get.'

Kipper was already sweating, but did all he could to increase his speed.

'I don't know if I can keep this up for very long. Please be as quick as you can, Tom.'

'All right, all right!' said Tom, from behind the goggles. 'I'll go as fast as I can, but it's pretty difficult operating this doll. You just concentrate on pedalling!'

Tom adjusted a knob at the end of one of the levers strapped to his arm.

The doll started shaking as its wings began to beat, then it slowly rose from the floor. Arthur watched as it wobbled and tried to keep upright. The lights from the doll's eyes flicked around the dungeon.

Its wings began to beat, then it slowly rose from the floor

The doll began to fly more steadily. Then it moved slowly across the corridor towards the gaoler. As it reached him, it slowed to a wobbly hover over the pocket.

'Oh my Gawd! I feel sick!' barked Tom. He moved his feet to try and steady the doll. 'That's it! I can see the pocket. But we need to lose height! How do I do that?'

'Kipper, you gently ease off the power,' ordered Grandfather. 'Tom, you will have to tell him when you start to fall, and when he needs to increase his pedalling.'

Kipper looked up at him and nodded his head. 'I shall enjoy easing off!'

The doll steadily descended till it was just an inch or so above the pocket.

'Steady, Kipper, steady!' whispered Tom. He moved the levers in his hands very slowly and the doll moved forward till its arms entered the pocket.

'A little more power, Kipper!' said Tom, and he started to manipulate the levers attached to his arms, concentrating as hard as he could. For a few moments there was silence as he struggled to make the precise movements he needed. Then, suddenly, he gave a triumphant shout.

'Got them! Now, Kipper, give it everything you've got!'

Kipper began pedalling ever more furiously, wheezing and panting with the effort.

The doll rose and the keys lifted from the pocket. Tom shifted the controls and the doll turned towards Arthur's cell.

'Please, get this done as quick as you can, or I am going to pass out,' moaned Kipper.

'Stop complaining, Kipper!' snapped Tom.

'Oh my Gawd! Something is happening!' said Kipper in a panic.

'Shut up and pedal!' shouted Tom.

William and Willbury were more concerned. Smoke was starting to rise from where the pedals joined the pump.

'Quick! Get the keys to the cell!' Grandfather shouted.

'What's happening?' asked Kipper. 'I'm going as fast as I can.'

There was a crunching noise, and the pedals seized.

'It's bust!' shouted Grandfather. 'Quick, before it dies!'

Smoke was starting to rise from where the pedals joined the pump

In the cell, Arthur had watched mesmerized as the doll had retrieved the keys. Now he stood horrified and helpless as it started to fall towards the floor. Tom pushed both of the levers in his hands forwards as far as they would go, and the doll tilted forward and dropped into a dive. As it neared the floor Tom pulled the levers back and the doll pulled out of the dive and rushed towards the cell door. Arthur stared in horror. If only it could keep going until it got to him—but it didn't look as if it was going to make it.

Now he stood horrified and helpless as it started to fall towards the floor

The doll hit the ground about two feet from the cell. In Grandfather's cave, Tom made one last frantic effort with the levers. Just as it hit the floor, the doll let go of the keys and seemed to propel them desperately towards Arthur. They slid across the floor and through the bars. Arthur picked them up, then reached through. He could just stretch far enough to retrieve the motionless doll.

'Grandfather! Grandfather! I've got the keys!' Arthur whispered in delight, but no one heard him. The doll was dead.

They slid across the floor, and through the bars

Very wet and miserable!

Snatcher and the other Members had been wading around for hours

Chapter 5

THE TRAPS

Snatcher and the other Members had been wading around for hours, and were very wet and miserable. First they'd checked the traps close to the elevator, but when they'd found nothing in them, they'd had to go further afield to check their other traps. Water was everywhere, running over the floor, running down the walls, and gushing from the ceiling. And the sound of it was so loud they had to shout to make themselves heard.

'Maybe we already got all the monsters down 'ere,' shouted Gristle.

'Well, you remember what I said. You don't want to find yourself in reduced circumstances do yer?' Snatcher replied.

'I think we should check the traps near the elevator again then . . . ' Gristle replied.

They made their way back towards the elevator. As they approached one of the traps Gristle smiled.

''Ere, guv. We got some!'

''Ere, guv. We got some!' and he pointed to a large net full of boxtrolls.

'My word, we struck it lucky. And some of them is big 'uns!'

Over the next few minutes they lowered the net and bundled their haul into sacks. Then they set off to check the next trap leaving a trail of vegetable teeth floating in the water. To Snatcher's delight and surprise, the next trap was also full of boxtrolls.

'Cor! You can never have enough size!' he shouted as he rubbed his hands together. 'Get them down, boys! I'm starting to enjoy this!'

The members bagged up the boxtrolls and moved on. At each trap they found more.

'This is blooming marvellous!' Snatcher chuckled. Gristle had never seen him so happy. 'Makes you wonder where they all bin hidin'—we ain't seen so many for weeks! Right lucky for us, but unlucky for them . . . and Ratbridge!'

'Ain't we got enough now?' asked Gristle, struggling under the weight of a sack.

'Oh, go on. Let's just check one more trap. It ain't going to hurt.'

'It's killing my back,' complained Gristle.

'That ain't nothing to what it's going to do to Ratbridge!' chuckled Snatcher.

*'Ain't we got enough now?' asked Gristle,
struggling under the weight of a sack*

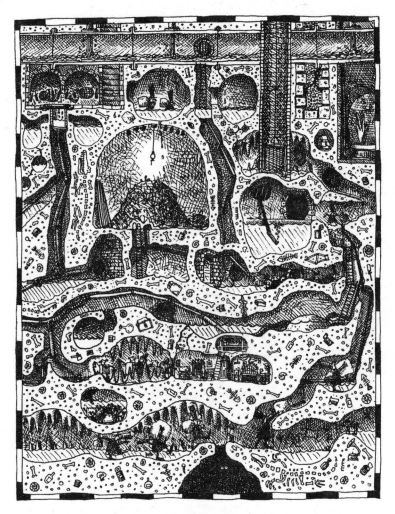

The Underworld

'No,' replied Grandfather, looking rather glum

Chapter 6

DEEP WATER

Willbury looked at Grandfather and sighed. 'I guess we don't know if Arthur got the keys.'

'No,' replied Grandfather, looking rather glum.

Just then Fish rushed into the room with Titus following behind. Fish started gabbling to Willbury.

'I don't understand,' said Willbury. 'I will have to get Titus to translate.'

He bent over and listened to Titus. Slowly he turned pale.

'Fish says that the water is starting to bring down the tunnel roofs. We had better get out of here quick.' Willbury paused for a moment. 'I think we should get back to the boxtroll nest to see if the others have found the elevator.'

Then he turned to Grandfather. 'You had better come with us.'

Kipper and Fish took Grandfather's arms

'Anything to get out of this damp. My bones are killing me,' said Grandfather.

Kipper and Fish took Grandfather's arms and led him out of the bedroom, with the others following. When they reached the living room Grandfather looked around.

'I shall rather miss this place,' he muttered.

'We better be quick or God knows what's going to happen,' urged Willbury.

Willbury grabbed a lantern and they set off towards the boxtroll nest as fast as they could through the water, which was starting to turn to a brown muddy soup.

When they reached a junction in one of the passages they had used to get to Grandfather's they had to stop. The tunnel ahead was flooded.

'What do we do now?' asked Willbury. 'We can't go back.'

Grandfather looked worriedly towards Fish. 'Do you know another route?'

The tunnel ahead was flooded

Fish thought for a moment then pointed to a side passage rather nervously. It too was flooded, but the roof of the passage was somewhat higher than the tunnel ahead.

Fish started to whimper.

'What's the matter, Fish?' asked Willbury.

Titus tugged on Willbury's cuff, and Willbury leant down to listen to him.

'Oh, dear!' muttered Willbury.

'What is it?' asked Grandfather.

'Fish is scared. It's the idea of having to swim. Boxtrolls loathe swimming. It is bad enough that they get their boxes wet . . . but swimming.'

Kipper waded towards Fish and smiled. 'How about I hold you up as high as I can so you can keep dry?'

Fish did not look convinced. In the distance there was another rumble and the sound of rushing water grew louder.

'Right, Fish. Close your eyes.' And before Fish could protest Kipper picked him up, and swung him above his head.

'Any room for a small one?' Tom asked hopefully.

'Go on, then, climb on board,' said Kipper, raising his eyebrows. Tom scrambled up to join Fish, then Kipper

Kipper carrying Fish, Tom, and Titus

turned to Titus. 'You may as well hitch a ride. One more is not going to hurt.'

Titus looked at the passage ahead, then with Willbury's assistance struggled up to join Tom and Fish.

Willbury looked concerned. 'I think I can manage with Grandfather, but the lamp?'

'I can take that,' said Tom, and Willbury passed the lamp to him.

'Do you think you will be all right, Kipper . . . carrying that lot?' asked Willbury.

'With all the exercise I get carrying washing?' he said and winked at Willbury.

Kipper turned and waded into the tunnel ahead and Willbury followed with Grandfather.

The water was very cold and Willbury felt his box go soggy as he hauled Grandfather through the water.

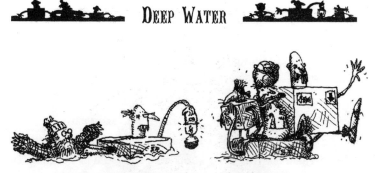

*Kipper turned and waded into the tunnel ahead
and Willbury followed with Grandfather*

'Are you all right?' asked Willbury.

'I could do with a warm bath, but don't worry,' said
Grandfather quietly, then he smiled.

Soon the water grew less deep as the passage angled
upwards and they made their way to a point where the water
became shallow.

'Do you mind if I have a breather,' puffed Grandfather.

'Let's climb up on that rock for a few minutes and rest,'
said Willbury pointing to a large flat rock that was still above
water. Everybody climbed up, looking forward to sitting
down for a moment. But before they could even catch their
breath, there was a twang, and they found themselves
hanging in a net from the ceiling.

'No!' cried Willbury. 'It's one of Snatcher's traps.'

There was nothing they could do but hang there and wait.
Wet and miserable, they huddled in silence, too dejected even
to talk. It was a few minutes before lights started to appear.

'You keep quiet and pretend to be boxtrolls,' Grandfather
whispered to Willbury, Kipper, and Tom. 'I think they'll be

taken in, even though you're not wearing your teeth any more. I'll have to take my chances.'

They fell silent as the Members approached.

Willbury saw Snatcher grinning from ear to ear.

'This one's full too!' he called back to the struggling Members. 'Sack this lot up, me lads, and we'll call it a day.'

The net was lowered onto the rock and the quarry inspected. There was a cry from one of the Members. ''Ere, guv. There's an old man in here with the monsters!'

'Well I never,' said Snatcher, leaning over Grandfather. 'If it ain't me old school friend William Trubshaw!' Then he grinned. 'So this is where you've been hiding all these years. It's typical of you to be mixed up with all these wretched underlings.'

'If it ain't me old school friend William Trubshaw!'

'Archibald Snatcher,' hissed Grandfather. Some of the Members close by heard this and giggled under their breath when they realized that Archibald was Snatcher's first name. Snatcher turned round and fixed them with a steely gaze.

'You think Archibald is funny, do you?' They fell silent. 'Shove him in a sack like the rest of them.'

Then he leaned over Grandfather again. 'You just wait till I get you back to the lab! By the time I've finished with you, you'll be wishing you were doing time for attempted murder instead!'

Members returning with their quarry by 'Cupboard'

Tea and cake

Chapter 7

THE SHAFT!

Snatcher stood by the open cupboard doors watching as the last of the Members dragged their wet sacks into the tearoom. Flashes of lightning threw shafts of light through the cracks in the boards over the windows and across the floor. Outside the rain fell hard on the streets of Ratbridge.

'Take 'em straight down the lab and chain 'em to the railings. It'll make it easier for sticking 'em in the "Extractor" . . . Then we'll 'ave a quick cup of tea and some cake.'

The Members picked up the struggling sacks and hiked them off to the lab. There they emptied the sacks out, chained the contents to the railing as ordered, and returned to the tearoom.

Willbury looked around the railing, and recognized all his fellow prisoners. There were the crew of the laundry, Marjorie and the boxtrolls Arthur had rescued, Fish, Shoe, Egg, and Titus, and finally Grandfather. Everybody looked rather battered and very miserable. The ones that had dressed up as boxtrolls now had broken or missing vegetable teeth.

Willbury noticed that Marjorie was anxiously studying the large funnel that hung above them.

Willbury looked around the railing, and recognized all his fellow prisoners

'What is that thing, Marjorie?' he whispered.

Marjorie looked very forlorn. 'They have done it! They've built a copy of my machine . . . only much, much bigger.'

'I thought you said it had two funnels?'

Marjorie pointed. 'See the small one over there, on top of the cage by the shed?'

'Yes,' replied Willbury.

'I think that is where they put the underlings to shrink them,' said Marjorie.

'And the big funnel up there?' asked Willbury.

Marjorie looked at the large doors in the floor. 'I'm not sure . . .'

They heard footsteps approaching from the entrance hall and they put their teeth back in. The duck stick appeared followed by Snatcher and the Members, all wearing their ceremonial robes. Snatcher made his way across to the control shed, climbed up the steps, went in, and then spoke through a trumpet device.

The duck stick appeared followed by Snatcher and the Members

'Tonight, gentlemen, we have a special show. Not only do we have enough monsters to finish our project, but also as a finale we shall for the first time use the machine to extract the size from humans. Please get the first boxtroll ready.'

Several of the Members descended on the boxtrolls. Marjorie was the nearest, and so they seized on her, unchaining her and pulling her across the room. She wailed and put up a good fight, but it wasn't long before the Members had her inside the cage with the door shut. The underlings were howling in despair. Willbury could stand it no longer.

It wasn't long before the Members had her inside the cage with the door shut

'Stop! This is inhuman.'

The Members turned to look. Snatcher came out of the control shed, and slowly walked down to where Willbury was chained.

'Human? What do you boxtrolls know about human?' Then he paused, and eyed up Willbury. 'Well, maybe you are a little more human than I thought!'

He put his good eye up very close to Willbury.

'I know you! You are that Willbury Nibble, that lawyer we've had so much trouble with. We've got your little friend locked up downstairs. I think I'll have him brought up so you can get shrunk together.'

Willbury froze. If Arthur had escaped then Snatcher had not found out yet! If he hadn't then the longer he stayed away from this machine the better. Either way, delaying Snatcher from sending someone down to get him was a good thing. He decided to change the subject.

He put his good eye up very close to Willbury

'This machine of yours is rather impressive. What are you using it for?'

'Wouldn't you like to know?' Snatcher grinned.

'It's not as if I can do anything about it. I'm sure your plan must be rather good.'

Snatcher puffed up a little as his vanity took over. 'You're right! You and your friends have already had your fate sealed so there can be no harm in telling you my plan. We are going to reclaim our rightful place as the overlords of Ratbridge. The Cheese Barons shall rule again!' And he laughed madly.

'So how are you going to do that?'

'This is what is going to allow us to do it. We are creating a Monster!' Snatcher paused for dramatic effect. 'And in part it's going to be with your help.' Snatcher laughed again. 'You know we have been shrinking your friends . . . well, have you wondered where the size goes?'

Willbury tried not to look worried.

'AH! You have! Well, I can tell you . . . the size is being put into a very special friend of mine, and as he gets bigger, he becomes more and more unstoppable!' Snatcher was now looking power crazed.

Snatcher was now looking power crazed

'Oh!' said Willbury. 'Your special friend . . . do we get to meet him?'

'Yes. Very shortly!'

'And . . . where does cheese come into all of this?' asked Willbury.

'The cheese! Cheese is central to it. To aid our monster's growth we have been force-feeding him a fondue of molten cheese. It goes down very well.' Snatcher guffawed. 'A DEEP WELL!' And he laughed at his own evil joke.

'Well, well,' said Willbury.

'Very droll, Mr Nibble. We have a heated pit that we drop cheeses into. This is piped directly to . . . the Great One. Right down his throat. I think 'e rather likes it.'

Willbury was horrified. What sort of monster could they possibly have created? 'So what happens now?' he said, playing for time.

'The boxtroll in the cage is about to donate some size to the Great One, and after that the rest of you is going to do the same. Then when you is all shrunk, and the Great One is finally the size we want, it's time to unleash him. Boy! Are we going to have fun! I hate this town!'

Snatcher turned and called for a ladder. Soon he was on the top of the shed waving his duck stick wildly in the air.

Soon he was on the top of the shed waving his duck stick wildly in the air

'To your places, gentlemen, we are about to start!'

The Members moved to positions around the lab tending different machines, and under Snatcher's feet, in the shed, sat Gristle at the controls. Great whooshes of sound filled the air as the beam engine started to move, then generators started to hum, and power surged through the sizing machine.

'Open the hatches!' Snatcher yelled above the noise.

Trout junior operated a winch in the roof that wound in the chains connected to the doors, while Trout senior took his place by the control panel on the rails and inserted a key. Soon the chains were groaning under the strain as they tried to lift the doors.

'More power, Little Trout!' shouted Snatcher.

Slowly the doors lifted and revealed a tiled shaft.

'Bring up the Great One!' screamed Snatcher.

Trout senior took his place by the control panel on the rails and inserted a key

Trout senior turned the key in the panel and a great creaking came from below. The Members stared towards the open shaft from their various stations, and everybody chained to the railings pulled back.

The creaking grew loud, and there was another sound, a hissing, sluggish breathing. It grew louder, as whatever it was rose up the shaft. Willbury and the others strained on their chains but it was no good. Their chains were fast.

Snatcher moved to the front of the shed roof and started to peer down the shaft. From his high vantage point he could see whatever was coming. He looked up at Willbury and laughed in a menacing way.

'You are about to meet my creation, Nibble. For all your meddling, it's done you no good. See what I am about to unleash on the world!'

Everybody chained to the railings pulled back

A huge bloated creature, larger than an elephant

What looked like a huge jelly covered in filthy grey matted carpet started to emerge from the shaft

Chapter 8

THE GREAT ONE!

What looked like a huge jelly covered in filthy grey matted carpet started to emerge from the shaft. As it did the smell of fetid cheese engulfed the lab.

Higher the great grey jelly rose, wobbling as it came. Something very long and rope-like was attached to one side of it, and on the other side . . .

Willbury stared as a pair of hairy door-sized ears came into view.

'It really is a monster . . . '

The ears were followed by great, red, dinner-plate sized eyes. They swivelled about wildly.

Willbury stared as a pair of hairy door-sized ears came into view

'No, it couldn't be!' cried Tom.

Still the creature rose. Its snout, bent and hairy, appeared.

Tom was jibbering. 'No! It can't be. It just can't!'

There was a loud clunk and the platform stopped as it reached the top of the shaft. Before them in all its glory was the Great One. A huge bloated creature, larger than an elephant.

'What is it?' wept Willbury

'I . . . I . . . I think it's a rat,' moaned Tom. 'And I think it's . . . Framley.'

'YES! What was once Framley is now . . . the Great One!' cried Snatcher. 'Once just nasty . . . Now made monstrous by the hand of man!' Snatcher broke into hysterical laughter for a few seconds, then he stopped, and turned to look directly at Tom.

'I'd been looking for someone really nasty, and when I saw dear sweet Framley in action I realized what a perfect subject he would make.'

'I . . . I . . . I think it's a rat,' moaned Tom. 'And I think it's . . . Framley.'

Tom was looking ill as his gaze darted between the Great One and Snatcher.

'Now you will witness the fulfilment of my dream.' Snatcher stamped on the roof of the shed and shouted. 'Extract the size!'

Snatcher stamped on the roof of the shed

At the controls in the shed, Gristle threw a lever.

Willbury blinked as there was a flash of blue light from the cage. He realized he could no longer see Marjorie. Then he heard another cry from Snatcher.

'Gristle! Give the Great One what he needs!'

There was another flash, but this time from the large funnel above, and the Great One wobbled.

Snatcher called out another order. 'Next, please! I think we will have the boy from the dungeon.'

'No!' screamed Willbury and Grandfather, as one of the Members set off in the direction of the dungeon.

'Oh yes! You'll enjoy watching!' laughed Snatcher, then he called after the disappearing Member, 'And can you bring back one of those shoeboxes down there. We need something to put all our friends in.'

'You're going to pay for this!' Willbury shouted.

'Quiet!' replied Snatcher. 'Or I'll turn up the voltage and you'll all be reduced to the size of ants!'

Willbury fell silent.

Snatcher spoke again. 'Get the little creature out of the cage.'

Willbury watched as Trout senior left his post by the railings, opened the door of the cage and groped about the floor inside. Then he stood up with something in his hands.

'What shall I do with it?'

'Perhaps Mr Nibble would like to be reunited with his friend?' Snatcher joked. 'Show him to the lawyer.'

Trout senior walked around to where Willbury was chained and held out his hands.

Standing there was a new tiny Marjorie, about seven inches high, and looking very unhappy.

Standing there was a new tiny Marjorie,
about seven inches high, and looking very unhappy

'Are you all right?' asked Willbury.

'Yes!' came a squeak. Marjorie looked startled by the new sound of her own voice. Then she squeaked again. 'I should never have built the prototype! I just never foresaw the consequences.'

Trout senior looked surprised at the little talking boxtroll in his hands, and lifted it up to take a closer look. Just as Trout realized who it was, Marjorie kicked him right in the eye. Trout screamed and dropped Marjorie on the floor, where she ran under one of the machines.

'Get back to your post!' Snatcher ordered Trout. 'We'll let the hounds find it later.'

Trout skulked off. Willbury looked about to see if he could see where Marjorie had gone, but he couldn't see her anywhere.

'Please, please find somewhere safe to hide,' Willbury muttered to himself. 'I couldn't bear it if you were eaten.'

'Now where is that blooming kid?' boomed Snatcher, as he looked towards the dungeon.

Trout screamed, and dropped Marjorie on the floor,
where she ran under one of the machines

A struggling Arthur appeared, being held by the scruff of his under-suit

There'd been quite a lot of noise from the dungeon

Chapter 9

THE NEXT VICTIM!

There'd been quite a lot of noise from the dungeon, before Snatcher heard heavy footsteps coming up the stairs. A struggling Arthur appeared, being held by the scruff of his under-suit. His captor was rather shorter than Snatcher remembered.

'Oi!' shouted Snatcher. 'You've forgotten the shoebox. Bring the boy here, then go and get it.'

As the Member led Arthur through the machines, loud metallic footsteps reverberated around the lab. Snatcher looked puzzled.

Grandfather and Willbury watched in despair as Arthur appeared by the pathway. Arthur and the Member froze at the sight of the Great One, and Willbury and the others chained to the railings.

'Come on! Come on! We haven't got all night. Get a move on!' ordered Snatcher.

The Member guided Arthur along the pathway towards the shed. As they passed, Arthur was looking worried, but winked, and Grandfather noticed the Member was wearing a mask and was holding something under his ceremonial robes. They stopped on the pathway before the shed.

'What you waiting for?' snapped Snatcher. 'Shove him in the cage, and go and get a shoebox.'

'No,' snapped the Member. 'Get your own shoebox.'

Snatcher was gobsmacked. No Member had ever answered him back.

'What!' he screamed. 'Me! Get my own shoebox?'

'Yes, Archibald!' replied the Member. 'Get your own shoebox!'

Snatcher went red with rage, and almost fell off the roof.

'You . . . ' Snatcher screamed, as he waved his duck stick at the truculent Member, 'are Expelled!'

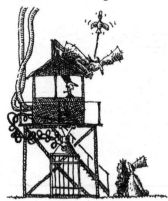

Snatcher went red with rage, and almost fell off the roof

Suddenly the Member released his grip on Arthur, and threw off his hat and robe. Standing by Arthur was Herbert in his iron boots . . . with his walloper.

The Members froze and Snatcher went very pale.

'Oh my God, he's out! Get him!' ordered Snatcher.

The Members didn't move.

'Get him!' screamed Snatcher. Still the Members held back as they'd all had experience of the walloper, and weren't willing to get within range.

Snatcher was starting to panic. ' . . . all right! . . . all right! . . . Break out the weapons!'

The Members rushed towards a large cabinet on a wall of the lab.

Grandfather shouted to Herbert. 'Smash the railings!'

Herbert looked back at Grandfather and grinned. Then he raised the walloper and brought it down hard.

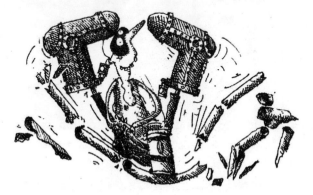

Then he raised the walloper and brought it down hard

There was an enormous crash as a section of the railing shattered. The blow was so hard that the Great One started to wobble violently, and let out an awful low moaning. Some of the boxtrolls were freed, and Herbert moved on to the next section. There was another blow and the Great One let out a huge bellow.

'Faster!' screamed Snatcher at the Members, who'd reached the cupboard, and were fiddling with the keys.

With two more blows all the railings lay shattered, and the prisoners freed. Willbury watched as Arthur ran to his grandfather, and hugged him. Willbury smiled for a moment, then turned and shouted to Herbert.

Willbury watched as Arthur ran to his grandfather, and hugged him

'Could you bash a hole in the wall so we can get out of here?'

Herbert looked serious. 'Where I wallop is me own business!' Then he winked at Willbury, and made for the wall opposite the cupboard where the Members were now arming themselves with blunderbusses.

Snatcher screamed, 'They're going to get away! Open fire!'

Willbury heard the first shot, and bits of broken cutlery flew over his head

Willbury heard the first shot, and bits of broken cutlery flew over his head. The Members didn't yet have clear sight of the escaping prisoners, as there were so many machines in the way.

'Follow me!' Willbury shouted. 'Kipper, can you help Arthur get Grandfather out of here?'

Kipper saluted, and ran to where Arthur was helping Grandfather. They took him by both arms, and set off after Willbury.

Herbert reached the outer wall and set about creating an exit. Within seconds a large hole appeared. He turned back to see Willbury approaching followed by the others.

Herbert reached the outer wall and set about creating an exit

Willbury guided the escapees through the hole

'Would you like it any bigger?'

'No,' smiled Willbury. 'I think it is big enough. An elephant could get through it.'

Snatcher was getting frantic, and dancing about on the roof of the shed in rage.

'They're escaping! Shoot them!'

Volleys of marbles, nails, bits of china, even old boiled sweets, clattered against the wall of the lab as Willbury guided the escapees through the hole.

'Make for the laundry!' he shouted.

The last out were Kipper, Arthur, and Grandfather. As soon as they were in the street Willbury turned to Herbert.

'Can you bring down the wall?' Willbury asked.

'A pleasure!' Herbert took a good long look at the wall, and swung his walloper.

There was a dull thump, and for a moment Willbury thought it hadn't worked. Then, cracks ran up the wall and a low rumbling started.

'Let's get out of here!' shouted Willbury.

Masonry crashed down as the wall collapsed, sending out huge clouds of dust.

As the dust settled all that could be heard was the sound of rain and distant iron socks on cobbles.

Iron socks on cobbles

*Willbury and Herbert caught up with Kipper and Arthur just
as they were helping Grandfather up the gangplank*

Tom and the captain came forward to meet them

Chapter 10

HOW ARE WE GOING TO FIX IT?

Willbury and Herbert caught up with Kipper and Arthur just as they were helping Grandfather up the gangplank. The Squeakers had gone, the dummies on deck had stopped dancing, but the crows were still very happily playing the harmonium. They hadn't got much better.

Reaching the deck they were greeted by the sight of all the other escapees. Tom and the captain came forward to meet them.

'Is everybody all right?' Willbury asked.

'I think so,' Arthur smiled. 'But where is Marjorie?'

Willbury looked glum. 'I forgot about her in the rush. I think she must still be trying to hide somewhere in the lab.'

'What are we going to do then?' asked Arthur.

'I think we will have to go back and get her.' Willbury

sounded a little reluctant. 'We also have to try to save Ratbridge from Snatcher and Framley.'

'How are we going to do that?' asked the captain.

'I don't think we have any choice but to take them on, and the sooner we do, the less damage they will have had time to do to the town.'

'We better be quick about it then,' said the captain. 'I don't really know how we take on Framley now he's so monstrously big, but I suppose we do have to try.' He turned to the crew and gave the order. 'OK! Gather all the weapons you can find!'

'Can we take off these stupid boxes?' asked Bert.

Fish, who was close by, looked very offended.

'I'm sorry,' apologized Bert, 'but damp cardboard . . . it chafes my legs!'

'OK. Everybody get changed!' ordered the captain.

Kipper raised a hand. 'May I keep my box on?'

'Oh! . . . If you really want to!' replied the captain. Fish smiled at Kipper who smiled back.

'And would you get me out of these darn socks?' pleaded Herbert.

Kipper went and found a cold chisel. He held it against the hinges of the boots, and with two careful blows of Herbert's walloper the socks were off.

Willbury looked at Herbert's feet. 'I think you had better go and wash those in the canal . . . And, Kipper, can you see if you can find some tin snips. Herbert needs to cut his toenails.'

He held it against the hinges of the boots

Shortly afterwards, when Herbert and Kipper returned, everybody was ready.

'Do you need shoes?' asked Willbury.

'Nah! After years in those socks, me feet are as hard as granite! And by the way you need some new tin snips.'

'And by the way you need some new tin snips'

'Herbert,' said the captain. 'I think we would like you to lead the assault.'

There was a cheer, and Herbert smiled.

Then Mildred came forward. 'Is there any chance us crows could come too? We could play you all into battle.'

Everybody went quiet, and then the captain spoke. 'I think it would be a good idea if you gave us a rousing send off, but somebody has to have the important job of looking after, and er . . . ' The captain paused and raised an eyebrow. ' . . . entertaining Grandfather and the miniature underlings.'

There was another cheer. The crows returned to the keyboard and started to try to play a march.

The crows returned to the keyboard and started to try to play a march

Arthur turned to his grandfather. 'Do you realize that now that Herbert is free, you have a witness to what happened? We could clear your name . . . And live above ground.'

'Yes, Arthur, maybe we could. But first we need to worry about Archibald Snatcher and whatever it is he's up to.' He smiled for a moment, and then he looked more serious. 'I'm not going to stop you from going back with the others to the Cheese Hall, but please think about it.'

Arthur looked him squarely in the face. 'I think I have to go back. I am not sure what's going to happen but I need to be there.'

'All right, Arthur, but . . . '

'I will be careful!' Arthur smiled. 'I haven't come this far to . . . well, you know?'

'Yes, I know,' said Grandfather, and he winked. 'Go on. Off with you!'

Arthur looked him squarely in the face

'Careful now, we don't want to hurt Baby'

A smile spread over Snatcher's face

Chapter 11
LET'S HIT THE TOWN!

As the clouds of dust settled, a smile spread over Snatcher's face. There was a huge hole in the wall of the lab.

'I was wondering how we were going to get the Great One out of here.' Then he snapped out an order. 'Ready the armour!'

Some Members ran to a corner of the lab and pulled dustsheets from a strangely shaped heap. Beneath the covers was a set of iron war armour. It looked like a cross between a giant snail shell and an old riveted boiler. A cannon was fixed above a small platform on either side, and on top in the centre of the back was another platform for the Great One's master to ride into battle upon.

Beneath the covers was a set of iron war armour

Inside the shed Gristle fiddled with some levers, and a crane moved across the floor to the armour. A hook was lowered from the crane, the Members attached it to the armour, and the armour was lifted from the floor. The crane moved towards the Great One.

'Careful now, Gristle, we don't want to hurt Baby.'

The armour slowly lowered, and the Members manoeuvred it over the rat. Snatcher climbed down from the shed and inspected the armour for fit.

'It's a bit loose around the edges,' Snatcher muttered. 'We really did need the extra size from those wretched underlings.'

Then he turned and cried, 'Gristle, could you lift the armour off for a moment . . . and could the Trouts please go into the cage, and check that the extractor funnel is correctly positioned . . . I am not sure it's working properly . . . '

The armour was lifted off, and the Trouts made their way into the cage. Snatcher followed, but stopped outside the door. Then in a blink, Snatcher snapped the door closed, and locked it.

'Shrink 'em, Gristle!'

The Trouts looked horrified. 'But Masterrrrrrrrrrrrr . . . '

There was a flash from above the cage, and the Trouts' cries grew higher and higher pitched, until only an indecipherable squeaking could be heard. Then there was another larger flash from the funnel and Framley wobbled again.

'That should do it!' said a satisfied Snatcher. 'Can we try the armour for size again?'

When the armour was back on the rat, Snatcher inspected it for fit again. 'Marvellous!' he chuckled. 'I knew he'd grow into it.'

The Great One now looked fearsome. The Members took the ladder from the shed and put it up to the platform on the back of the rat. Snatcher climbed up, and a couple of the Members climbed onto the platforms on either side.

Snatcher climbed up

'Right, me lads. Gather round.'

The Members assembled, and Snatcher spoke from his seat, perched high on top of the rat.

'Members of the new Cheese Guild, the time is here!'

There was a loud cheer.

'The Great One is ready, and Ratbridge is going to pay!'

There was an even louder cheer.

'Yes, my brothers! We shall use our Leviathan to overthrow those that have held us down for so long. First we shall remove their government, then destroy the banks, smash their factories, and return Ratbridge to follow an open free trade in cheesy products!'

There was a silence, and then Gristle raised a hand. 'Eh . . . what do you mean?'

'We're going to use the big rat to clobber them what done us down, blow up the council offices, rob the bank, knock down the factories, and then start flogging dodgy cheese again!' Snatcher replied.

There was an enormous cheer.

The Members followed carrying their blunderbusses

'Right! Let's hit the town!' shouted Snatcher, and he took hold of a pair of reins that had been fixed to the mouth of the Great One, and pulled hard. Slowly his war machine rose and turned towards the broken wall. The Members followed carrying their blunderbusses.

'I've been looking forward to this.' Snatcher smiled to himself.

'Right, what's the plan?' asked the captain

Herbert leading the way with his newly fresh feet

Chapter 12

ATTACK ON THE CHEESE HALL

Herbert led the way through the streets of Ratbridge. The sun was rising and was just breaking through under the dark storm clouds, and their footsteps were mixed with the rumble of thunder and rainfall. As Willbury surveyed the little army, he wondered about their selection of weapons. Some of the pirates carried large pants, and were accompanied by rats carrying the notorious gunge balls. This he understood, but the others . . .

The boxtrolls had selected screwdrivers and adjustable spanners, Titus had found a small trowel and a bucket full of gravel, and the other pirates and rats seemed to have grabbed anything that was handy—mops, buckets, old fishing rods, in fact anything that took their fancy. Willbury carried an umbrella that was keeping him dry, and that he thought might be useful in a fight, while Arthur walked by his side carrying the doll.

The thunder drew closer as they stood in front of the Cheese Hall in the rain.

'Right, what's the plan?' asked the captain.

Kipper smiled. 'Perhaps Herbert could "open" the front door for us, and we could creep in that way and surprise them?'

'I don't think there will be much surprise after the noise of Herbert walloping down the door,' said Arthur.

'If we wait for a flash of lightning, count a few seconds, then Herbert wallops the door, the thunder will mask the sound of the wallop,' suggested Tom.

'That is a very intelligent idea!' Willbury agreed, and smiled at Tom.

They waited for a minute or so until the next flash came. Willbury held up a finger, counted for a few seconds, then gave the signal to Herbert. At the very moment the walloper struck the door, a loud clap of thunder filled the street. The front door was reduced to matchsticks and everybody waited to see if the Members were going to come rushing out to meet them. After another minute there was still no sign of them.

'I think we got away with it,' said Kipper.

'Right! Get the mobile knickers ready,' ordered the captain.

Pairs of pirates stretched knickers between them, rats loaded them with the gunge balls, and each pair of pirates was joined by a third pirate who stretched the knickers back ready for firing.

'Everybody keep quiet and follow the knickers,' ordered the captain.

Slowly, the pirates with the loaded knickers made their way up the passageway towards the entrance hall and the others followed. As they reached the archway to the hall, one of the leading pirates peeked round the corner, and signalled that nobody was there. The little army made its way into the entrance hall.

Slowly, the pirates with the loaded knickers made their way up the passageway towards the entrance hall

'Prepare yourselves,' whispered the captain. 'I think Herbert should wallop the lab door, and then we let off a volley of knickers . . . ' But before he could finish, the lab door started to creak open and everybody froze.

Around the bottom of the door a tiny person appeared. It was Marjorie.

'I wondered when you were going to get here,' she squeaked. 'But you're too late. They've gone!'

There was a mixture of surprise, relief, and worry.

Around the bottom of the door a tiny person appeared

'Thank God you are all right,' said Willbury to Marjorie.

'I am not hurt, but all right is not exactly how I feel,' squeaked a sad-looking Marjorie. 'Six inches tall . . . ' Her voice trailed off.

'Well, I am not sure we can do anything about that right now,' said Willbury sympathetically. 'I think we'd better stop Snatcher and the Members before they cause too much destruction. Do you know where they have gone?'

'They've taken the rat to wreak their revenge on the town. First they're going to destroy the Town Hall, then rob the bank, and after that they are going to destroy all the factories!' squeaked Marjorie.

Everybody looked shocked.

'We've got to stop them!' cried Willbury.

'But how?' asked Arthur.

'Knickers and a good walloping!' suggested Herbert.

The crew of the laundry gave a cheer.

'I don't think even that could stop them now,' Marjorie said to Herbert. 'They have equipped the rat with some really heavy iron armour and cannons. And from what I can see, that rat is vicious and afraid of nothing now he's enormous. It's going to take something really powerful to stop them now.'

Everybody fell silent, then after a few moments Arthur spoke.

'Did you say "iron armour"?'

'Yes,' replied Marjorie.

'The same stuff that Herbert's boots were made of?'

'Yes. Why?' Marjorie asked.

'I am not sure if it would work, but I have an idea,' Arthur explained. 'There is a powerful electromagnet somewhere above the roof of Herbert's cell. When they wanted to stop him from attacking them, the Members would turn it on, and Herbert's boots would stick him to the ceiling. Couldn't we use that?'

Marjorie's eyes lit up. 'If it was powerful enough, it might work.'

Willbury looked perplexed, and turned to Arthur. 'I don't understand.'

'Don't you see? We could use the electromagnet!' said Arthur. 'If Framley is wearing iron armour, we could turn on the magnet, and pull him back here.'

'Yes . . . But is the magnet powerful enough?' asked Willbury.

'We could use the electromagnet!'

Marjorie smiled. 'It will be by the time I'm finished with it!'

Everybody cheered.

'Where was your cell?' Marjorie squeaked to Herbert.

'Just below us somewhere,' replied Herbert.

'Could you pick me up and show me approximately where?' Marjorie asked him. 'If we can find the spot just above your cell, we should be able to find the magnet.'

Herbert carefully picked up Marjorie and looked towards the stairs to the dungeon. Then he made towards a space behind the beam engine.

Arthur and the others followed. As Herbert rounded a corner, Marjorie let out a squeak.

'Here it is!'

There was a very large coil of wire on a cart.

Willbury looked puzzled. 'Are you sure? It's just a large coil of wire.'

'YUP! That's what it is until you put electricity through it,' Marjorie squeaked with glee. 'Now all we have to do is put enough electricity through it to give that rat a surprise!'

There was a very large coil of wire on a cart

'What do you want us to do?' asked the captain.

'Well, when we turn it on, we have to make sure the rat comes to the magnet, rather than the magnet going to the rat. If we make sure there is something really solid between the coil and the rat, that should stop it moving,' squeaked Marjorie.

'How about the end wall of the lab . . . and it is closest to the Town Hall,' suggested Arthur.

'Good idea,' said Marjorie.

'What about all the machinery in here?' asked Willbury. 'Won't the coil be attracted to that?'

'Mmmmmm! You have got a point. We'll have to fix the magnet to the wall. Some of the loose parts of machinery might fly towards it, but the heavy stuff is fixed down firmly, I think.'

Fish made a gurgling noise, and Titus came forward to whisper to Willbury.

Willbury spoke. 'Titus says the boxtrolls are very good at that sort of thing and would like to help.'

'Very good!' Marjorie squeaked, turning to the boxtrolls. 'You lot move the coil and fix it to the wall.'

The boxtrolls smiled, and Shoe made a burbling noise.

Titus whispered to Willbury, and Willbury passed on the question to Marjorie.

'I don't really understand, but they would like to know if you would like them to rewire the cabling so you can have the switch up here rather than down in the dungeon.'

'Bless me! That would be grand,' squeaked Marjorie. 'Could we have the switch in the control shed, please? And wire the coil directly to the generators?'

Shoe nodded, and the boxtrolls set to work. Then Marjorie turned to the captain.

'We need as much power as possible if we are going to stop that rat,' squeaked Marjorie. 'Do you think your crew could stoke up the boiler as fast as you can? The beam engine that powers the generators will have to be running flat out.'

'Be our pleasure!' said the captain. 'We know all about stoking boilers.'

So the crew of the Nautical Laundry set to stoking the boiler of the beam engine. The boiler was still hot, so it

didn't take long before the great arm of the beam engine was pumping up and down, and the flywheel was spinning again.

Marjorie asked Willbury to carry her up to the shed, and Arthur and Titus accompanied them. As they entered Willbury looked about. On the bench at the back of the shed were Arthur's wings and the strange device with two small funnels.

The strange device with two small funnels

Willbury pointed to it. 'Is that yours?'

Marjorie looked rather awkward. 'Yes . . . Yes, it is.'

Arthur was not paying any attention to them as he was checking his wings.

'At least they haven't had time to take them apart again,' he muttered to himself.

Willbury put Marjorie down on the control panel. She took a few moments to study the controls, then pointed to one of the dials.

'That shows the pressure in the steam boiler.' Then she pointed to a lever. 'And that lever engages the generators. Arthur, could you swing it to the upright position, please?'

Arthur obliged. As soon as he did, a gentle whirring started and built to a loud hum that filled the whole lab. A needle in another large dial in the control panel started to climb.

Arthur thought for a moment then asked Marjorie a question. 'How did they make the magnet work when the beam engine wasn't running?'

'Arthur, you really are as sharp as a knife.' Marjorie smiled. 'You saw all those glass tanks?'

'Yes,' replied Arthur.

'Those are batteries. They store power, but not enough for what we want. That's why I asked the boxtrolls to wire the coil directly to the generators,' answered Marjorie. 'Now all we have to do is wait until the needle hits the red.'

'Are you sure that's safe?' asked Willbury.

'Er . . . no,' confessed Marjorie. 'But it should be all right . . . for a bit . . . '

The stokers were doing their work well; the beam engine kept increasing in speed and the generators hummed louder. Soon the needle reached the red.

'Arthur, can you tell the boxtrolls to stand clear of the magnetic coil, please?' asked Marjorie.

Arthur leant out of the door and shouted to the boxtrolls. 'We are going to turn the magnet on. Stand clear!'

Arthur was surprised that the boxtrolls immediately dropped all their tools and ran to the other end of the lab as fast as their legs could carry them. He turned to Marjorie.

'They're clear!'

'Well then,' Marjorie squeaked to Arthur. 'Would you like to throw the switch?'

Arthur looked a little uncertain.

'Don't worry. What can happen?' smiled Marjorie.

Arthur paused for a moment, and then threw the switch.

Every piece of loose metal in the lab flew towards the magnet. Tools, nuts and bolts, pieces of machinery, the door handle of the lab, bits of chain, and several enamelled mugs and plates whizzed past fearful heads, as they made the most direct way to the magnet, where they formed a jumble on the surface of the coil.

'Strong, isn't it?' Marjorie smiled.

'Strong, isn't it?'

At the head of the procession rode Snatcher high on the back of Framley. Following were the other Members, carrying an assortment of blunderbusses and other weapons, and behind them ran the cheese-hounds.

Shutters were thrown open by the townsfolk to see what all the commotion was

Chapter 13

MAGNETISM!

Ratbridge was a strange town and had seen some very strange and fearful sights during its history, but none as strange and fearful as that which made its way through its streets now.

At the head of the procession rode Snatcher high on the back of Framley. Following were the other Members, carrying an assortment of blunderbusses and other weapons, and behind them ran the cheese-hounds. Sparks flew out from below Framley's belly as his armour grated on the cobbles of the streets. The noise drew people from their beds, and as the procession approached, shutters were thrown open by the townsfolk to see what all the commotion was. Very quickly the shutters were closed and bolted again.

Very quickly the shutters were closed and bolted again

Encouraged by the obvious fear they were generating, Snatcher chuckled to himself. He hadn't felt this good for years . . . or ever! Life felt wonderful.

'Just wait till I get to the Town Hall!' he giggled. Looking ahead his eyes fixed on a rank of shops. About halfway down the rank was a shuttered shop frontage with the three balls of the pawnbroker's sign hanging above it.

'I wonder . . . ?' he muttered to himself.

As Framley drew level with the shop front Snatcher pulled hard on the reins attached to Framley's jaws. The Great One stopped. Snatcher turned to the Members who had come to a sudden halt behind him. And spoke.

'I am sorry, lads, but I can't resist it!' He then pulled on Framley's reins and aimed the rat at the front of the shop. 'Go on, my beauty! Let's see what you can do.'

For a moment the rat didn't move, then realizing just how big he was and just how small the shop looked, he raised his head and swung it at the front of the shop.

The shop did not put up much of a fight. Within a fraction of a second the shutters and windows gave way and the contents of the windows spilled out. The Members let out a mighty cheer and ran forward to gather up the treasures now strewn across the street.

'This is going to be so easy!' shouted Snatcher. 'Help yourselves, boys, there is going to be plenty more where that came from.'

Snatcher pulled on the reins and set the mighty rat off

The shop did not put up much of a fight

again towards the market square. As they made their way through the streets he set Framley upon several more unfortunate shops that took his fancy, and each in turn was reduced to a wreck in seconds.

Finally they arrived at the market square, and crossed it to arrive outside the Town Hall. Snatcher brought the procession to a halt, and turned to the Members.

'This is where the real fun begins, lads! Prepare to charge!' Snatcher shouted.

Gristle, who had made his way to the side of the Great One, now spoke up. 'Can't we use the cannons? I likes a bang. Please, please let's use the cannons.'

Snatcher looked down at Gristle and smiled. 'Oh all right, Gristle. As you have been so good. We'll use the cannons.'

Then Snatcher gave the order. 'Prepare to fire!'

The Members who were standing on the platforms on the sides of the rat took out boxes of matches, and the other Members levelled their weapons at the front of the Town Hall.

'Ready . . . Fire!' Snatcher cried, as he brought down his arm.

There was a roar of cannons and blunderbusses . . . but then something very strange happened that seemed to defy the laws of nature. The cannon balls, and the nuts and bolts that the Members had fired, hurtled towards the Town Hall, then very rapidly slowed . . . stopped . . . and turned back towards the Members.

A Member with a box of matches

'Duck!!!' screamed Snatcher. The Members hit the floor as the missiles whizzed over their heads and continued back across the market square in the direction of the Cheese Hall. Everybody looked very baffled.

'Prepare to fire!' Snatcher screamed again.

The Members tried to follow orders but now their guns and ammunition seemed to want to go home, and were pulling the Members back towards the Cheese Hall.

'Master . . . ' cried a very frightened Gristle. 'Something weird is 'appenin' . . . '

The Members hit the floor as the missiles whizzed over their heads

Their guns and ammunition seemed to want to go home

'Stand firm!' ordered Snatcher, but the terrified Members were now letting go of their blunderbusses, and untying their ammunition bags from their belts to avoid being dragged across the square.

'Load the cannons!' cried Snatcher. The two Members on either side of the rat unstrapped cannon balls from the platform floors, but before they could load them into the cannons found themselves dragged off the platforms, and disappeared across the square, screaming.

'It's a curse!' cried one of the Members.

'Run!' cried another. And the Members ran in all directions.

Across Ratbridge many people were just getting up, and might well have been very frightened by the noise of the blunderbusses and cannons, if it were not for the thunder, and the fact they had problems of their own. In every household, objects were coming to life.

Saucepans and cutlery had suddenly decided to stick to walls, and cooking ranges and iron bedsteads were going for walks. Several ladies who had slept in their steel reinforced corsets now found themselves irresistibly drawn to join the saucepans and cutlery. One man who had invested in an expensive set of metal false teeth found himself hanging on as tightly as he could to the kitchen table to avoid being dragged through the house, while outside in the street, dogs with studded collars found themselves sliding through the mud towards the Cheese Hall.

Snatcher looked completely flummoxed. A cart, riderless bicycles, garden furniture, and several old barrels were all making their way at high speed across the market square. Snatcher looked down at the head of the great rat.

Snatcher looked completely flummoxed

'It's down to us, Framley! Attack!' And Snatcher pointed towards the Town Hall.

The Great One let out a low moan.

'Come on, my horrid!' cried Snatcher.

Framley seemed very perturbed. His legs were scrabbling on the wet cobbles, but he and Snatcher were not moving forward . . . in fact, they were starting to slip backwards . . .

Inside the lab Arthur and the others were feeling a little nervous about the strange noises that were coming from outside. They seemed to conform to a pattern. All seemed to start with a distant whizzing or clattering that grew louder very quickly, then stopped suddenly with thwonk, thud, or similar.

'Do you think we'd better go and have a look at what's happening?' Arthur asked Tom.

'I think we know what's happening, Arthur. For the time being I think we'd better stay safely in here. If the metal doesn't get us, I think there are going to be some very angry people out there,' Tom replied and then winked.

Snatcher turned around to see the last of the cannon balls break from their lashings and fly off across the square. The rat was picking up speed, despite desperately trying to cling on to the cobbles with its claws. There was a horrible scraping and grinding as the armour slid across the market square.

'Oh, my poor horrid!' Snatcher muttered. Framley just let out a mournful whimper.

On the way to the Town Hall Snatcher had taken what he thought was the most direct route, but he now discovered that there was an even shorter route back . . . a straight line.

As the armoured rat reached the edge of the market square, it was not a street that they met but a cobbler's shop. Snatcher could see what was going to happen and crouched down on the back of the ever-accelerating rat and hung on.

The shop, like most of the buildings in Ratbridge, was badly built, and put up little opposition.

There was a crashing and they disappeared through the shop frontage, leaving a large armoured-rat-shaped hole. In the apartment above the shop where the cobbler lived, there was much surprise as a screaming crouched man on a small railed platform came through the wall, moved rapidly across the room, and out through the back wall. The Great One then slid across the muddy back garden till it reached the next building, and disappeared again.

There was much surprise as a screaming crouched man on a small railed platform came through the wall and moved rapidly across the room

The armour protected Framley as they smashed through badly-built building after badly-built building, but Snatcher was getting rather bruised. And all the time they were picking up speed.

Finally, with a great deal of splintering and crashing of masonry, Framley broke from a cake shop across the road from the lab, shot across the street, and hit the lab wall in a puff of flour and cake crumbs.

The building shook.

'I think someone's arrived!' Marjorie squeaked, then Herbert giggled.

Willbury spoke to Arthur. 'Can you get up to one of the windows and see what's happened?'

Arthur ran down to the floor of the lab and found a wooden stepladder, placed it below a window near the magnet, and climbed up. After a few moments he turned and shouted.

'It's Snatcher and the rat! And they both look really angry . . . '

'We'd better keep them there then,' replied Willbury.

Arthur took another look out of the window. 'I'm not sure you want to do that!'

'Why?' shouted Willbury.

'Because Framley is being squashed by his armour. He could burst at any moment!'

'Can we just reduce the strength of the magnet, Marjorie?' asked Willbury.

Marjorie looked unsure. The stokers were still very enthusiastic, and the generators were spinning faster and faster.

'The circuit is either on or off. The only way we can ease the power off the magnet is to slow down the generators, and that's going to take a few minutes even if we stop stoking the boiler and let off some steam . . . !'

'Framley is being squashed by his armour. He could burst at any moment!'

'Quick!' shouted a very worried-looking Arthur. 'Framley looks like he could blow any second . . . '

Willbury turned to Marjorie. 'Well?'

'We could turn the current off for a few seconds . . . ' Marjorie suggested.

'Do it!' snapped Willbury.

'Herbert! Can you lift me up so I can turn off the switch?' Marjorie squeaked.

Herbert lifted Marjorie to the switch and she tried to grab it. The switch was red hot and Marjorie jumped back.

'Let me try!' shouted Herbert. And he leant forward and again pulled back from the red-hot switch.

'I can't! It's too hot.'

Marjorie jumped back

Willbury wrapped a handkerchief around his hand and tried. It was useless . . . with all the current the switch had fused solid.

'We have to get everybody out of here!' cried Willbury. 'An explosion could bring down the rest of the lab.'

Willbury grabbed Marjorie and ran out of the shed followed by Herbert and Titus, and then he shouted from the top of the stairs.

'Everybody out! Run for your lives! Don't use the hole in the wall! It's too close to the rat! Use the door to the entrance hall.'

Willbury, Titus, the stokers, and boxtrolls all ran for the entrance hall, but as Willbury reached the door he turned to see Arthur making for the shed.

'Arthur! What are you doing?' he shouted.

'I've got to get my wings,' Arthur shouted back.

Arthur ran up the steps to the shed and in through the door. He grabbed his wings and hastily strapped them on. Then he grabbed Marjorie's prototype from the bench, and made for the door. As soon as he was outside he wound the handle on the wings' motor as fast as he could. He had never wound it as fast in his life.

Over the noise of the machines in the lab he heard Willbury calling him from the door to the hallway.

'Arthur! Arthur!'

Arthur turned to see the last of the underlings and laundry crew disappearing out of the door past Willbury.

Arthur adjusted the knob on the front of the box, pressed both buttons, and jumped.

*Arthur adjusted the knob on the front of the box,
pressed both buttons and jumped*

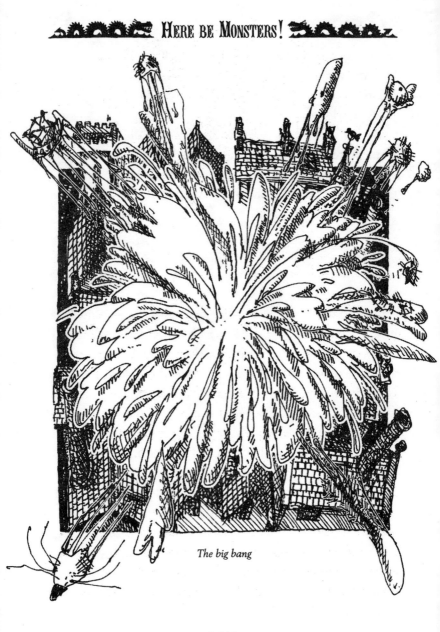

The big bang

The day was not going well for Snatcher

Chapter 14
THE BIG BANG

The day was not going well for Snatcher. His attempt to return himself to his rightful social position seemed to have failed; the Members had all run away; he'd been dragged through a number of buildings; and now it was raining water from above and small metal objects from every other direction. How could things get worse?

Beneath him the iron shell that had protected the giant rat was now looking rather battered and flimsy. The Great One was being squeezed and was bulging out round the edges of the armour like a squashed balloon.

Then it happened.

Framley had not eaten since he'd had his last dose of 'size', and even though he was extremely uncomfortable he felt rather hungry. There on the ground right beneath his head, in the midst of a pile of rubble and cake crumbs, was a

*There on the ground right beneath his head,
in the midst of a pile of rubble and cake crumbs, was a cream bun*

cream bun. It was not a large cream bun, but it would do until he could get more cheese. He reached down, snapped up the bun, and swallowed. What followed was disastrous.

A clap like thunder broke as Framley burst and everything went yellow!

A cream bun

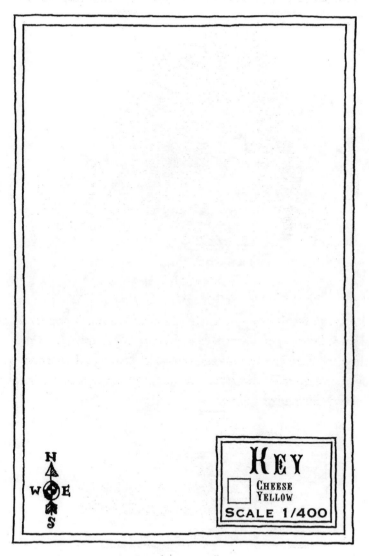

N
W E
S

Everything went yellow!

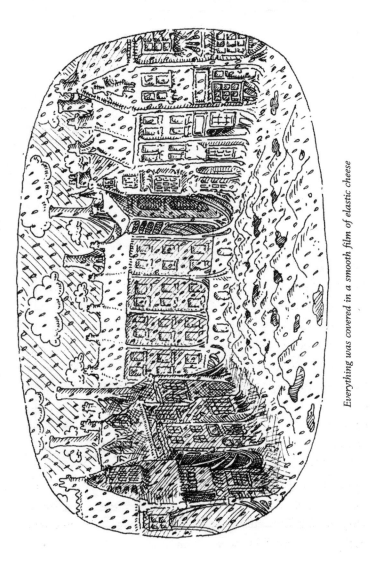

Everything was covered in a smooth film of elastic cheese

The two mice in the bottle

Chapter 15

SKINNED!

Arthur flew straight towards the lab door where Willbury stood waiting. When Willbury was sure Arthur was coming, he turned and ran. Arthur followed.

Just as Arthur was about halfway across the entrance hall, he remembered the two mice in the bottle. He turned and landed by the door of Snatcher's suite, ran in, grabbed the bottle from the table, ran back out of the door, and then across the hall through the archway. As he ran down the passageway to the front door he was hit by a blast from behind.

The blast shot him through the door, and as he saw the front windows of the inn approaching rapidly, he felt someone grab him out of the air and pull him to the ground. Then he felt himself covered by something thick and very sticky, and everything went silent.

Arthur tried to stand up. He was under some kind of soft elastic yellow tent. With a slight struggle, he freed his hands, and then with one finger he managed to poke a hole through the yellow skin. With a little difficulty he stretched the hole until he could step out of it. Strands of cheese hung from his wings.

With one finger he managed to poke a hole through the yellow skin

He was standing in a shiny yellow street. Arthur looked about. Everything was covered in the smooth film of elastic cheese. He turned towards where the Cheese Hall had once stood. Now there was just a low, shiny, yellow mound. The buildings around the Cheese Hall all now had yellow frontages, but didn't seem to be damaged (apart from the bakery).

Then Arthur remembered the others. He looked about on the ground close to where he stood. Odd shapes were wiggling under the cheese skin, and some were just starting to break through the film. Close to where he stood was the form of Willbury, laid flat with outstretched arms. Arthur ran and started to peel the cheese film away from his friend.

'Willbury . . . Willbury . . . Are you all right?' Arthur cried.

Arthur tore at the cheese

A muffled grunting came through the skin. Arthur tore at the cheese and soon he had Willbury freed.

'Thank you, Arthur!' said Willbury as he tried to disentangle cheese strands from his wig. 'We'd better help get everybody else out.' Then he stopped.

'Have you seen Marjorie?'

'No!' replied Arthur. 'When did you last see her?'

'I think I let go of her when I grabbed you.'

They looked down at the smooth film that covered the cobbles. Arthur couldn't see any shape that could be Marjorie, and then he turned towards the inn. In the middle of the front door was a perfectly formed moulding of their friend.

'Look!' cried Arthur, pointing at the door. Willbury ran over and unpeeled her.

She gave a splutter. 'I hate cheese!'

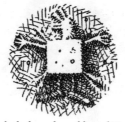

A perfectly formed moulding of Marjorie

Within a few minutes, everybody was unpeeled and had gathered together. They all looked rather shocked, but happy, apart from the captain and the boxtrolls. The boxtrolls' boxes were now so damaged by the rain and the blast that they were embarrassed to be seen in them.

Arthur remembered the bottle and ran to where it lay, still under the cheese. He broke through and saw that the bottle was smashed. Close by, the bodies of the two tiny mice lay on the ground.

'Captain! Quick, over here!' Arthur called.

The captain rushed over and looked.

'I think it's Pickles and Levi!'

'You're right . . . I would recognize them any size,' said the captain. 'But they're not moving . . .'

The captain picked them up and looked at them very closely

The captain picked them up and looked at them very closely. 'They are not quite the right shape though . . . sort of swollen up around the belly . . . and there seem to be strands of cheese around their mouths.' His eyes lit up. 'And they're breathing!'

Levi and Pickles started to move and let out little groans.

'They must have gorged themselves on the cheese,' the captain said, smiling, and then carefully placed them both in his pocket.

'What do you think has happened to Snatcher and Framley?' asked Arthur.

'I think we can guess what has happened to Framley,' said Willbury, surveying the cheese. 'But Snatcher? I think we'd better go and look for him.'

Willbury led the group over the mound that had once been the Cheese Hall, towards the place where the back wall of the lab had stood. Large pools of water were now collecting on the surface of the cheese. They reached the street on the far side of the mound, and started to look about for signs of Snatcher.

Willbury led the group over the mound that had once been the Cheese Hall

After about half an hour, they were just about to give up when a new noise started. It was a low rumble and they could feel it under their feet. Beneath the town, the water had been doing its work. The foundations below the Cheese Hall had been almost completely washed away and, combined with the shock from the explosion, it was just too much. The rumbling grew louder and the earth began to shake. Arthur turned towards the mound and noticed ripples running over the surface of the pools of water.

'Look, Willbury! Look at the water!' Everybody turned to stare.

'Quick!' shouted Willbury. 'Get back from the mound!'

The rumbling was growing louder, and they could see that the mound was starting to shake.

Having retreated quickly, they just stood and stared as there was a huge cracking noise and the mound suddenly disappeared.

'Look, Willbury! Look at the water!'

In the same moment, all across the town, the iron plates covering the holes to the Underworld were blown high into the air, and in the woods the trotting badgers were shot out of their tunnels, and were last seen flying over the next county. Fortunately for the rabbit women, the doors they had constructed to keep the rabbits in were very well built, and saved them from the blast.

Quiet returned and everybody moved forward to look down the hole. It was some twenty or thirty feet deep and lined with the skin of cheese. Water was washing about in the bottom.

'It's a big hole!' said Kipper. 'If it was blue it would look like a swimming pool.'

'What's a swimming pool?' asked Arthur.

Willbury smiled. 'I think we had better get back to the ship to see if your grandfather and the others are all right. Kipper can show you what a swimming pool is later.'

'It's a big hole!' said Kipper

Then Willbury noticed how forlorn the boxtrolls looked.

'I am sure we can find a few new boxes; if not I shall have you some made!' The boxtrolls beamed, as they had never had brand new boxes.

'It's all very well for them,' said Marjorie. 'But what about me, and the other shrunken creatures?'

'Hang on a minute!' said Arthur, remembering the prototype. He rushed back around the edge of the hole to where it lay under the cheese skin. After a few seconds he managed to break through the skin and retrieve Marjorie's machine. Arthur lifted it up carefully, and then ran back to where the others stood.

As he arrived back at the group he heard Marjorie squeak with delight. 'Oh, Arthur, thank you, you've got my sizer!'

Willbury took the sizer from Arthur, and gave it a long look, and then spoke. 'I don't want to disappoint you, Marjorie, but where do you suggest we get your size back from now that Framley is no more?'

Marjorie looked glum. 'I hadn't thought of that . . . '

'There must be somewhere to get it from,' said Arthur.

'Where do you suggest we get your size back from now?'

'Maybe,' said Willbury. 'We'll have to think.'

As they set off for the ship the townsfolk were just arriving to find out what all the commotion was. They formed small, very puzzled, silent groups that gawped at the newly decorated hole and buildings. The underlings had been through so much that now even Titus held his cabbage up in a very un-cabbagehead way, and walked straight past them.

What nobody noticed was that high above, just under the gables of the bakery, was what looked like a ship's figurehead of a very angry man wearing a top hat. The figurehead started to slide slowly down the wall.

The figurehead started to slide slowly down the wall

She swooped down to meet them

They saw a crow flying towards them

Chapter 16

REPAIRING THE DAMAGE

Weary, and covered with bits of sticky cheese, but feeling proud and relieved, the group began to make its way back to the laundry. As they did so, the rain stopped, and they saw a crow flying towards them. It was Mildred. She swooped down to meet them, and circled a few feet above their heads.

'What's happened?' she cawed. 'We heard an explosion and a big crunch a little while later.'

Everybody smiled, and Willbury spoke. 'We got Marjorie and Levi and Pickles back, and we stopped Snatcher.'

'Is everybody all right?' asked Mildred.

'I think so!' said Kipper. 'Well . . . Marjorie, Levi, and Pickles are still little . . . '

Marjorie gave an unhappy squeak.

'And Framley blew up!' added Arthur.

'That was the explosion you heard,' said Tom. 'We are not sure about Snatcher. He disappeared.'

'How did Framley explode?' Mildred asked.

'It's a long story,' said Willbury. 'I think it best if we get back to the ship, then everybody can hear it.'

'I'll fly back and tell them you're coming,' said Mildred.

Arthur had an idea. 'If you'll wait a moment I'll join you.'

Mildred looked surprised, and watched as Arthur stopped and wound the box on his front. After a minute or so they heard the ping, and Arthur unfolded his wings.

'Cor! Like your wings,' said Mildred. 'What are those bits that look like cheese on them?'

'Cheese!' giggled Kipper.

'What are those bits that look like cheese on them?'

Arthur crouched down, jumped, and pressed a button. Mildred flapped out of the way as Arthur rose up to join her.

'We'll see you in a few minutes!' Willbury called after Arthur. 'And get the cocoa on!'

Arthur followed Mildred up above the rooftops and back towards the laundry. The streets were filling with people and many of them turned to stare up at Arthur as he flew over.

'Ain't they seen anybody fly before?' cawed Mildred.

They were joined by the other crows

Arthur smiled. It was magnificent flying over the town by day, and with all the rain there had been the air was clean and clear. As they approached the laundry, they were joined by the other crows. Arthur spotted Grandfather below, on the deck, and waved. Grandfather waved back and Arthur could see him smiling.

'Get the cocoa on!' said Arthur as he touched the deck. 'The others will be back any minute.'

Grandfather came forward and gave him a hug.

'It's good to see you in one piece!'

'Not bad to see you either!' chirped Arthur.

Grandfather released him. 'We had better get the cocoa on. The milkman has been, and there's plenty of hot water as the boiler was on all night.' Grandfather chuckled.

'We'll get the stuff,' cawed Mildred. 'Give us a hand, Arthur.'

She led the way below decks to the galley, and they returned just in time to see the others returning. Soon everybody was sitting on deck grinning, swapping stories, and drinking cocoa out of buckets. Even Marjorie seemed happier, and was fiddling with her prototype.

Then they heard a whistle from along the towpath, and everybody turned to look. It was the Squeakers.

'Goodness, will we never be given any peace?' sighed Willbury. He stood up and walked to the top of the gangplank to meet them, and everybody followed.

The Squeakers dismounted from their bicycles and took out truncheons and handcuffs. The Chief Squeaker approached the bottom of the gangplank carrying a large sheaf of papers. When he reached the gangplank he stopped, raised the papers in front of him, and spoke.

'I hereby arrest all presently residing upon this ship, formally known as the Ratbridge Nautical Laundry, under sections . . . ' He paused and shuffled through his papers. '. . . C35 . . . D11 . . . Y322 . . . T14 . . . W24b . . . W24b . . . Q56 . . . of the Ratbridge penal code. I also charge you with . . .' And he looked at his papers again, 'riotously destroying a grade six public building, escaping custody, playing music without licence, causing a disturbance between the hours of 11 p.m. and 6.30 a.m. . . . and about fourteen other charges . . .'

Willbury raised a hand. 'I think, sir, that it ill behoves one who has assisted in kidnap and wrongful imprisonment, handled stolen goods, aided in a plot for the destruction of the official offices of this town, been a member of an illegal organization, connived with those who have been illegally hunting cheese and have been experimenting on animals without a licence . . . to cast the first stone.'

'I hereby arrest all presently residing upon this ship'

The Chief Squeaker looked puzzled. 'What do you mean?'

'I will explain it in court!' snapped Willbury. 'And while we're at it, I have another case to talk to you about.' He turned and waved Grandfather and Herbert forward.

'Do you remember a case many years ago where a man was poisoned with Oil of Brussels in a local hostelry?' said Willbury, addressing the Chief Squeaker.

'Yes. I'd just joined the police, and it was the first crime scene I ever attended. Very nasty case. We chased the assailant but he disappeared,' the Chief Squeaker replied.

'Well, do you remember that one of the witnesses also disappeared?'

'Yes—Archibald Snatcher said he had gone home for tea . . .'

'I think, sir, that it ill behoves one. . .'

'Was it not lunchtime? And was this not the man?' Willbury pointed to Herbert.

Herbert grinned, and the Chief Squeaker gave him a funny look.

'It could be . . .'

'I am telling you it was. This man was knocked unconscious and imprisoned by your good friend Archibald Snatcher, and has languished in a miserable cell under the Cheese Hall ever since, to stop him from giving true evidence.' Willbury paused for a moment and fixed the Chief Squeaker with his gaze. 'It was Archibald Snatcher who was responsible for the poisoning. Yes! That very same Archibald Snatcher, whom we all witnessed you investing with legal powers to justify a kidnapping and aiding in the theft of a pair of mechanical wings. I intend to sue whatever remains of the Cheese Guild on behalf of my clients here, for compensation, and I am sure the full story will come out.'

The Chief Squeaker went very pale. 'Umm . . . Er . . . I think there might have been a misunderstanding . . .' He lowered his papers. 'Didn't you say you had retired?'

'I was retired but I now feel that it is my duty to return to the law,' replied Willbury.

'Oh!' muttered the Chief Squeaker and then turned to the other Squeakers. 'Back to the nick . . . Quick!'

Everybody on the deck of the ship cheered as they watched the Squeakers disappear down the towpath.

'You're rather good at this law thing,' Arthur said to Willbury.

Willbury grinned, and turned to Grandfather. 'I think it's going to be safe for you to set up home above ground now if you would like to.'

'Thank you,' said Grandfather, and he shook Willbury's hand.

Everybody on the deck of the ship cheered

The deck of the Ratbridge Nautical Laundry

Snoozing in the morning sun

Chapter 17

HOME

On deck everybody had finished their cocoa, and with the Squeakers sent off with their tails between their legs, there was an air of relaxation. Some of the crew were disappearing below deck to get cleaned up, while others were snoozing in the morning sun. Willbury wandered across to Arthur and whispered quietly to him.

'I think that your grandfather is very tired. It would be a good idea if he had a rest and time to recover. Why don't you and Herbert take him down to the captain's cabin, and look after him, while I get a few things sorted out.'

'All right,' replied Arthur as he turned and looked fondly at his grandfather. Then Arthur turned back to Willbury looking a little worried. 'I don't like to ask this but I am worried about where we are going to live, and—'

Willbury cut him off. 'You are not to worry about that.

I have an idea. You concentrate on looking after Grandfather. I am sure he has missed you and it would be good for both of you to catch up.'

Arthur smiled and walked over to where Grandfather and Herbert were chatting.

'Willbury says we're to get you down to the captain's cabin so you can have a rest, Grandfather.'

'Oh, all right. If I have to! I am feeling much better though, now that it's stopped raining and my bones have had time to dry out.'

'Come on!' chuckled Arthur, as he and Herbert helped Grandfather to his feet and then across the deck to the stairs down to the cabin.

He and Herbert helped Grandfather to his feet then across the deck

For the rest of the day Arthur sat by Grandfather, listening to stories of Herbert's and Grandfather's youth. There didn't seem to be anything wrong with Herbert's memory now as story after story unfolded, and Arthur could hardly bear to tear himself away from them, but they kept needing fresh top ups of cocoa and biscuits from the galley.

There were tales of learning to ride bicycles, disastrous experiments, of pet frogs and engineering projects.

By late afternoon they were all growing sleepy, when Grandfather turned and spoke to Arthur.

'I am glad we have come above ground. I loved every moment I spent living in the Underworld with you, but it's not the best place for a child to grow up in. You need sunlight, and you need friends. And now you are going to have both.'

Arthur smiled, and a quiet calm settled on the cabin.

About seven o'clock there was a knock on the cabin door and Arthur, Grandfather, and Herbert awoke to see Kipper's face, smiling and covered in splashes of paint.

'If you would like to come through, Willbury has called a meeting in the hold, and would like you all to attend.'

'Why have you got paint all over you?' asked Arthur.

'You'll just have to wait and see,' replied Kipper, as he turned and disappeared out of the door.

Herbert and Arthur went to help Grandfather up but before they got to him he had stood up on his own.

'Come on, then,' said Grandfather, 'what are you waiting for, let's get to the meeting.' And he set off. Herbert and Arthur grinned at each other then followed.

When they arrived in the hold Willbury was sitting behind the ironing board with the captain. In front of him lay the prototype resizing machine and Arthur noticed Marjorie almost hidden behind it.

Willbury saw Grandfather walking by himself and smiled. 'Would you like to join me here, Grandfather? There is a spare chair.'

Grandfather nodded and made his way to the chair while Arthur and Herbert joined Kipper, to sit amongst the boxtrolls. Arthur noticed that quite a few of the pirates and rats also had splodges of paint on them and that they were smiling at him. Then Willbury spoke again.

Splodges of paint

'My dear friends, there are a number of important issues to resolve, and I think it best if I outline them, then we discuss how they might be solved.' He turned to Grandfather. 'I have already taken the liberty of asking my landlady if she would rent the vacant rooms above my shop to you and Arthur. She agreed and this afternoon I had Kipper lead a working party to clean and repaint the rooms. There is even a small boxroom that Herbert could use till he gets his own place. Kipper tells me he has sorted out some basic furniture, so you are welcome to move in any time you like.'

Grandfather smiled from ear to ear and called to Arthur, 'What do you think?'

'Yes, please!' answered Arthur with a huge grin. Kipper and Fish both patted him on the back.

There was a roar of approval from the meeting and then Grandfather spoke. 'I want to thank you from the bottom of my heart . . . but how are we to pay the rent? I don't have a job and I haven't got any savings.'

'You're not to worry about that. I have filed a claim for compensation, on your and Herbert's behalf, this afternoon with the clerk of Ratbridge courts, against Snatcher and the Cheese Guild. Until it comes to court, if Arthur helps out with chores, I'll sort out the rent.'

'I have filed a claim for compensation, on your and Herbert's behalf, this afternoon with the clerk of Ratbridge courts'

There was another cheer. Willbury raised a hand and spoke again. 'Now we come to our friends the underlings.' He turned to where the underlings sat.

'The problem of the entrances to the Underworld has been solved, but . . . ' He paused, 'at the moment most of the Underworld is flooded. Does anybody have any suggestions?'

Marjorie stood up on the table and squeaked, 'Easy!'

Willbury looked startled. 'Yes?'

'We already have a beam engine on this laundry. Pumping water is what they were built for. All we have to do is drop a pipe down into the Underworld and pump out the water.'

'I might be being stupid,' said Willbury, 'but where are we going to pump the water to?'

Marjorie looked flummoxed.

Marjorie looked flummoxed

Kipper raised a hand. 'How about the hole where the Cheese Hall was? That cheese seems to be pretty waterproof and would stop it leaking back into the Underworld.'

'Would it work?' Willbury asked Marjorie.

Marjorie thought for a moment. 'I think so . . . and once the underground becomes drier the boxtrolls could repair their drainage system to stop it flooding again.'

The boxtrolls made gurgles of agreement.

Kipper raised a hand again. 'Can I help them?'

'I see no reason why not,' Willbury said and turned to the captain, who was nodding in agreement. Kipper smiled.

'Well, that just leaves us with one last problem. Size! We have our friends here who have been reduced in size, but we know there are many others, and some in the hands of those who just treat them as pets. We have to get them back, and we have to work out where to get the size to put them right. Does anybody have any suggestions?'

'How about we find the Members what ran away, and suck the size out of them?' Bert suggested. There were cheers from the pirates and rats.

Willbury stood silently until the cheers died away. 'I'm sorry but I'll not countenance revenge shrinkings. We must not lower ourselves to that. No, we must find another way. Does anybody have any other suggestions?'

'Couldn't we use vegetables to suck the size from?' asked Tom.

Titus looked shocked, as Marjorie raised a hand to speak. 'It doesn't work. You have to use living creatures. If you used vegetables it would be very dangerous and you might end up with some strange results.'

'What, like half trotting badger, half potato?' asked Kipper.

'Yes,' replied Marjorie.

'Might be an improvement,' suggested Tom.

Half trotting badger, half potato

'I think we have to stick with getting the size from creatures,' said Willbury. 'But I am really not sure how.'

'Couldn't we all donate a little bit of size?' asked Grandfather.

'You could, but with all the creatures we have to resize it would leave you all pretty tiny if it were to make any difference,' replied Marjorie rather sadly.

'Well, let's think on it,' said Willbury. 'And there is the issue of how we get the other underlings back to resize them in the first place. They're in homes all over the town and we simply don't know where they are. If we do find them and just steal them back we are going to start another whole round of trouble, and with the court case coming up that is the last thing I want.'

The hold fell silent and everybody looked rather glum. After a few minutes Willbury spoke again.

'Let's get some rest. It has been a tiring few days, and I am sure we'll think better after some sleep. We can all meet up here tomorrow morning to start pumping out the underground. Marjorie, will you take charge of that?'

Marjorie nodded.

'Could those that are coming back to the shop meet me up on deck?' said Willbury.

The meeting broke up, and a few minutes later Arthur found himself on deck with the boxtrolls, Titus and the tiny cabbagehead, Grandfather, Herbert, Marjorie, and Willbury.

'Are we taking the little sea-cow with us?' asked Arthur.

'No, she is staying here for the moment. The crew have grown very fond of her,' Willbury replied.

They set off, and soon arrived at the shop. Willbury opened the front door and stopped in his tracks.

Willbury opened the front door and stopped in his tracks

'Oh, my word!' he exclaimed.

Before them was the shop but now it was cleaner and tidier than Willbury could possibly have ever imagined. The walls and ceiling had been given a fresh coat of white paint, the old bookshelves had been righted and repaired, and were tidily stacked with all his books, the floorboards had been swept and polished, and against one wall stacked soap boxes formed open-fronted storage spaces into which the rest of Willbury's loose possessions had been neatly piled up. His bed was freshly made and some extra blankets were neatly folded at the foot of the bed.

There was a popping noise and Willbury turned towards the fireplace. He smiled. In front of the fire was his old

*Before them was the shop but now it was cleaner
and tidier than Willbury could possibly have ever imagined*

armchair . . . and it also had been repaired.

Willbury turned round. 'Welcome home! Would you like to come in?'

The little group walked into the shop and Willbury closed the door, then took a key off his keyring and handed it to Grandfather.

'This is a spare key to the front door. Please feel free to wander through here whenever you like.' Then he turned to Fish.

'Would you like to show our friends their new home?'

Fish smiled at Arthur and led them through the door at the back of the shop into the hallway. Now it was Fish's turn for a surprise. Where once the hallway had been dark and dingy, it was now bright and clean. A lit ship's lantern hung from the ceiling, and every surface was painted white. Fish was just about to lead them up the stairs when he noticed there was something different about the back room as well. He ran down the hall and gave a gurgle. Arthur, Grandfather, and Herbert followed.

The back room looked like a new ironmonger's shop.

Cubby-holed shelving made from cardboard now covered the walls, and all the nuts and bolts that had been on the floor had been sorted and placed in different labelled holes.

Fish let out a whistle, then stopped still when he noticed a stack of folded ... clean ... brand new ... cardboard boxes on the floor. After a few seconds he walked forward slowly, and bent down to stroke the top box. Then he turned and let out an enormous gurgling cry.

He walked forward slowly, and bent down to stroke the top box

There was a scrabbling of feet from the shop and the other boxtrolls rushed past Arthur, stopped, and hooted at the sight of the boxes. The boxtrolls looked from the new boxes to each other then to Arthur, Grandfather, and Herbert.

Fish came forward and gently shooed Arthur, Grandfather, and Herbert out of the room and closed the door. As soon as the door was shut, there was a frantic tearing of cardboard, and whooping, followed by some chewing noises, then the door opened again. Fish and the other boxtrolls were wearing the new boxes and were grinning from ear to ear.

Wearing new boxes and grinning from ear to ear

Fish swaggered along the hall and marched up the stairs, waving for Grandfather, Arthur, and Herbert to follow. As they reached the top of the stairs Arthur ran ahead. There were three doors. He opened the first one and there was a tiny room with a hammock and another cardboard box. But this time the cardboard box had been tipped upside down to form a table. On it was a small vase of flowers and a cake.

'Is this my room?' he called over his shoulder.

'No, that is the boxroom for Herbert.' Arthur smiled and opened the next door. There he saw a brass bed, and to his surprise, tools laid out on a workbench.

'Is THIS my room?' he asked.

'No!' came Willbury's voice. 'It's Grandfather's.'

'Is THIS my room?'

Grandfather walked past Arthur and smiled. 'I do hope so.' He walked forward, looked at the bench, then sat on the edge of the bed and smiled a huge smile.

Arthur then turned to the last door. 'Then this MUST be my room!' He opened the door.

The room was a little smaller than Grandfather's and was painted completely white, including the floor. There was a cardboard box table like in the smaller room, but there were also some shelves. On the top shelf, lying on its side, was a large bottle. And inside the bottle was a model of the Ratbridge Nautical Laundry—complete with tiny washing. Arthur ran forward to look at it, and noticed a small plaque fixed to the bottle. Engraved on the plaque were the words, 'To Arthur from the R.N.L.'. Arthur beamed and turned to the others standing behind him.

Inside the bottle was a model of the Ratbridge Nautical Laundry

Herbert spoke. 'Kipper had been making it since they arrived in Ratbridge, and when he heard that you had lost all your toys, he decided you would make a good home for it.'

Arthur felt very touched. 'I shall treasure it always.'

Then Arthur looked about the room again. There was a hammock hung from corner to corner. Arthur jumped into

He was holding his doll

it and lay down. It felt very comfortable apart from a bump behind his neck. He reached his hand round and retrieved whatever was causing the discomfort. To his surprise he found he was holding his doll. Arthur was confused. He checked to see if he had another doll under his suit, but discovered it was not there.

He swung himself out of the hammock and ran next door to his grandfather.

'My doll? It was in . . . ah . . . my room!'

'Where else did you expect to find it?'

'I don't understand?'

'I think you dropped it when you were caught in the explosion. Tom found it and knew that it was broken . . . so he brought it to me. My eyesight is not so good these days and I asked Marjorie if she could fix it this afternoon.'

Arthur smiled and held up the doll.

'I'm afraid that it will never fly again, but you will be able to speak to me through it in a few weeks after I have got to grips with these new tools.'

They smiled at each other, and Grandfather spoke again. 'I think we are going to be happy here.'

'Cocoa!' came a call from downstairs.

'Yes . . . yes we are,' said Arthur.

They smiled at each other

Children swimming in Grandfather and Herbert's hole

Arthur helps with the pumping out of the Underworld

Chapter 18

MEASURE FOR MEASURE

The next few weeks were very busy for Arthur. Grandfather thought it would be a good education for him to help with all the work that had to be done, so each morning Arthur would set out for the laundry and help out. Some days, under the guidance of Marjorie, he would help the crew of the laundry pump out the Underworld, and on other days he would work with the boxtrolls as they rebuilt the underground drainage system. He enjoyed these days most as Kipper and Tom worked with the boxtrolls. Kipper still wore his battered cardboard box and now had learnt to 'speak' boxtroll. This made him very useful and happy.

While Arthur worked during the day, Willbury, Herbert, and Grandfather spent their time preparing the compensation case against Snatcher and the Cheese Guild. When the day of the trial came, neither Snatcher, nor any

Member of the Cheese Guild, turned up to defend themselves, and the court awarded the hole in the ground to Herbert and Grandfather (as it was the only property that Snatcher and the Cheese Guild owned).

That evening after dinner, everybody who lived in the shop went for a gentle walk to view Grandfather and Herbert's hole. As they approached it they noticed local children swimming in it.

'I think you are going to have to fence off your hole,' said Willbury. 'What would happen if a child got into difficulty?'

Herbert and Grandfather looked at the swimmers rather glumly.

'Seems a pity. I suppose we could pay one of the pirates to keep an eye on the kids . . . But where would we get the money to pay him?' said Grandfather. 'We still have not got even enough money to pay you rent.'

'Why don't you charge for admission?' asked Willbury.

Herbert and Grandfather agreed this would be a good idea, and Willbury advised them that it would still be a good idea to put up a fence, to stop any accidents. They all trooped off to the laundry and were greeted with friendly cries.

'Is the captain about?' Willbury asked Mildred, who had flown down to meet them.

'Yes! He's down in his cabin. You know the way.'

They made their way below decks and knocked on the cabin door.

There sat Tom with the captain's hat on, behind a huge heap of laundry slips

'Come in!' came a familiar voice.

Willbury opened the door and there sat Tom with the captain's hat on, behind a huge heap of laundry slips.

'What are you doing here?' asked Willbury.

Tom smiled. 'I got voted captain last Friday. It's rather nice but I am looking forward to next Friday. I can't stand the paperwork. Anyway, what can I do for you?'

Willbury explained and it was agreed that in exchange for half the profits the laundry would provide lifeguard cover every day between six a.m. and eight p.m., and that they would also help erect the fence around the pool. It was also agreed that any spare hot water left over from the laundry would be piped into the pool.

Soon the 'Ratbridge Lido' (as the pool became known) was the main attraction in the town. Children would swim there by day, and in the evening when it wasn't raining the fashionable women would parade along its shores, while the pirates would have raft races. Herbert, who enjoyed swimming very much, taught Arthur how to swim and once the water became warm, Grandfather could be found taking a dip most days.

The pirates would have raft races

All this time the question of the shrunken creatures had not been solved, but then something happened.

A Frenchwoman arrived in Ratbridge and found work in one of the cafés that had sprung up around the Lido. She immediately became the centre of attention for the fashionable women, as she was from 'Pari'.

For days the ladies spent their time plucking up courage to ask her questions about the latest fashions till finally one Ms Hawkins could bear it no longer and stormed into the café.

'May I ask you about the Pari fashions, my dear?' Ms Hawkins asked.

'Certainly. What do you want to know?' replied the Frenchwoman.

'Is it true that hexagonal buttocks are going to be the rage this year?' said Ms Hawkins knowingly.

'*Quel horreur!* What is it with zee Ratbridge ladies and their fascination for ridiculous buttocks?'

Ms Hawkins dropped her pet boxtroll and fainted. When she recovered she went straight round to her friend who wrote the fashion articles for the *Ratbridge Weekly Gazette*, and the following Friday a special edition of the paper came out with two main articles. The first was a report covering all the details of what Snatcher had been up to, and the second an article on the fact that buttocks were 'OUT!'

'*Quel horreur!*'

Next morning, as Arthur made his way to the laundry, he approached the towpath and discovered it was thronging with the ladies of the town. After a struggle he managed to

make his way past them till he reached the gangplank. Kipper and a number of the bigger pirates were holding back the crowd who were trying to get on the ship. Kipper saw Arthur, grabbed him and lifted him aboard. Here he found Tom and Marjorie looking very worried.

'What's happening?' shouted Arthur over the noise of the crowd.

'We are not sure, but it has something to do with my resizing machine. They have heard we have got one here,' squeaked Marjorie.

Kipper saw Arthur, grabbed him and lifted him aboard

'Quick! You've got to come and deal with them!' shouted Kipper. 'We can't hold them back for much longer.'

'What are you going to do?' asked Arthur.

'I don't know . . .' panicked Marjorie.

'Let one of them up here and see what they are after?' suggested Tom. 'It might be the only way to stop a riot.'

They all nodded and then Tom called out to Kipper to let one of the ladies through. Kipper did as he was ordered and a very cross looking woman strode up the gangplank, and as she did the din died down.

'How can I help you?' Marjorie squeaked.

'I've read that you have a machine like the one that Snatcher had, that can shrink things?' It was Ms Hawkins.

'Er . . . Yes?' Marjorie replied.

'I want you to shrink my buttocks! And that is not a request but an order!' said Ms Hawkins.

Marjorie looked astonished. 'Umm . . . Are you sure?' she squeaked.

'I am not leaving here till you do,' she replied. 'You can

use my boxtroll to put the size into,' she went on, thrusting
a tiny boxtroll towards Marjorie.

'I want you to shrink my buttocks!'

'All right, if you insist . . . ' Marjorie smiled. 'But I do
charge!'

'I don't care. I want my buttocks reduced at any price,'
Ms Hawkins insisted.

'How about ten groats a pound . . . and your boxtroll?'
Marjorie said.

'Done!' Ms Hawkins snapped, and took out her purse.
'Who'd want a big boxtroll anyway, it's only the small ones
that are fashionable!'

'Very well then!' Marjorie squeaked. Then she turned to
Tom and Arthur. 'Can you rig up a screen for the ladies and
take the money?' They nodded. 'We need something for
them to go behind and it needs a hole in it big enough for the
funnel on my resizer.'

Marjorie turned back to Ms Hawkins. 'I've got to go and get my machine, and while I am away I want you to go behind the screen and prepare yourself. When I get back I am going to put the funnel through the hole, and you must place a buttock against it. I'll extract the size, and then you'll have to place the other buttock against the funnel. When I have done that one, I'll upsize the boxtroll.'

Marjorie disappeared below deck, while Tom finished putting up the screen with the aid of the crows, and Arthur took the money. One of the pirates found a pair of scissors and cut a hole in the screen. Ms Hawkins huffed, placed the boxtroll on the deck, and then disappeared behind the screen.

Tom finished putting up the screen with the aid of the crows

Marjorie returned, struggling with her machine. 'Tom, can you get one of the pirates to operate the resizer? I don't think I am big enough.'

Tom found a volunteer and Marjorie ordered him to push the funnel through the hole in the screen.

'Are you ready? Please place your first buttock against the funnel!'

'Ready!' came the cry from behind the screen.

'Extract the size!' Marjorie ordered the pirate. The pirate pulled the trigger and there was a flash and puff of smoke from behind the screen. This was followed by a delighted titter.

'Please place your second buttock against the funnel!'

'Ready!'

'Extract the size!' There was another flash and puff of smoke and yet another titter of delight.

Ms Hawkins appeared from behind the screen to gasps of admiration from the women standing at the top of the gangplank. Where once her buttocks had stood, her figure was now as straight as a board.

Where once her buttocks had stood, her figure was now as straight as a board

With no word of thanks she marched past her fashion rivals, flaunting her non-existent buttocks, down the gangplank and disappeared.

Marjorie now ordered the pirate to point the other funnel at the tiny boxtroll on the deck.

'Do you understand what we are doing?' she asked the boxtroll. The boxtroll nodded and grinned.

'All right, release the size!' Marjorie ordered. There was another flash and instantly the boxtroll grew about three inches.

There was another flash and instantly the boxtroll grew about three inches

'Well done!' Marjorie said to the boxtroll, who was looking very pleased.

Over the course of the day many ladies were treated, including a large number who didn't have underlings as pets. This enabled Marjorie to get all the creatures back to their original size. There were cabbageheads and boxtrolls, and several women turned up with buckets containing fresh-water sea-cows. These proved a little more difficult to resize, as they had to be taken out of their bucket and kept wet

On deck there were swarms of full-size underlings

during the process, then gently lifted over the side and lowered into the canal.

By late afternoon Arthur had had to find somewhere to put all the money. He now had a large barrel almost full of banknotes and coins, while on deck there were swarms of full-size underlings.

There was still a queue of ladies on the towpath, but none of them had pet underlings.

'Where are you going to put the size?' asked Arthur.

'We need to find some more shrunken underlings,' said Marjorie.

'Shall I go and get Match from the shop, and the little cabbagehead that Titus is looking after?' Tom asked.

'Yes, and what about the fresh-water sea-cow that was here on the boat?' Marjorie asked.

'We did her hours ago,' Tom smiled.

'Well, what shall I do while I'm waiting? There are still loads of ladies on the towpath . . . '

'Isn't that obvious?' asked Tom.

'No,' replied Marjorie.

'Don't you want to get back to normal?' Tom asked.

'Of course. It had gone clean out of my head.'

Tom went off and returned half an hour later with

everybody from the shop, to see a full-size Marjorie standing on deck, accompanied by full-size versions of Pickles and Levi.

Marjorie grinned at Willbury as he arrived.

Marjorie grinned at Willbury as he arrived

'I am not sure I approve of this,' said Willbury.

'We didn't have much choice in the matter,' said a much less squeaky Marjorie. 'I think we would have been lynched if we had refused to co-operate. And look at all the underlings!'

Willbury looked around at all the happy big underlings standing around the deck.

He smiled. 'Well, let's finish this off. Fish, can you bring Match here? We are going to get his size back.'

Fish came forward and placed Match on the deck in front of the screen, and Marjorie ordered the pirate to let another lady through.

Over the next few minutes the queue of ladies on the towpath disappeared and Match and Titus's friend regained their size.

'That's the last one!' said Marjorie triumphantly. 'Everyone's back up to full size!'

'Right!' said Willbury. 'Marjorie, could you lend me your machine for a minute.' Marjorie looked curious, but handed the machine over. Willbury placed it on the deck.

'Herbert, could you do the honours with your walloper, please?'

'But . . . ' Marjorie cried and started to move forward to get her machine.

Willbury raised a hand. 'No! We have had enough of all this resizing. I am going to get Herbert to destroy the resizer and I want you to promise you are not going to try to build a new one.'

Marjorie looked rather sad. 'I suppose so . . . '

'All right then. Herbert, wallop the machine!'

Herbert walloping the machine

There was a mighty crash and the resizer lay bent beyond recovery on the deck.

'Thank you, Herbert!'

Marjorie stood staring at the ruins of her machine, while Willbury stared at the barrel full of money near Arthur.

'Don't complain! I think you have made rather a lot of money out of this. Perhaps you could put it to some more useful purpose than just changing the size of things.'

'And maybe something that causes less trouble,' added Grandfather, looking up at the smog that was starting to settle over the town. 'Have you ever thought about going into pollution prevention?'

'I did have an idea about how to distil oil and run a motor off it. It would be a lot cleaner than steam engines.' Marjorie grinned.

'Do you think I could help?' asked Arthur.

'Of course you could. I need an bright assistant.'

That night a party was held on the laundry. The crows played harmonium, vast quantities of cocoa were drunk, everybody danced, and complaints were made about the noise to the Squeakers, who did nothing about it. As the party died down, Arthur wandered onto the towpath with his friends Fish, Tom, and Kipper for a little peace away from the crows' music. As they walked along the bank they saw Willbury and Grandfather sitting on the bank with Titus.

'What are they doing?' asked Arthur.

That night a party was held on the laundry

'Looks like throwing weeds in the canal,' replied Kipper.

As they approached, Willbury put his fingers to his lips to keep them quiet, then pointed out into the canal.

There was the mother fresh-water sea-cow and her size-restored calves, feeding on the weed that Willbury and Grandfather had been throwing in.

They watched until the sea-cows had had their fill and had turned and swum off down the canal. Willbury and Arthur helped Grandfather to his feet and they all waved as the little group of sea-cows slowly disappeared into the distance.

'You know, for all its failings, I rather like Ratbridge,' said Willbury.

'It's not all bad, is it?' replied Grandfather as he gave Arthur a wink.